THE FAITH OF A CENTURION

DATHAN BELANGER

CLAY BRIDGES
P R E S S

The Faith of a Centurion

ISBN: 978-1-7352217-0-0
eISBN: 978-1-7352217-9-3

In loving memory of Irene (Gonsalves) Torres

TABLE OF CONTENTS

PREFACE

I wrote this book so readers could experience a fascinating story and learn the details of history they would not normally pick up from a history textbook. It is my hope that readers will come to understand a little more about the true circumstances of life in the first century during the time of Jesus. I firmly believe in the value of historical fiction, novels that echo the mistakes and triumphs of those who have come before us. These novels use interesting stories to show how circumstances affected people personally, deeply, and emotionally. Historical fiction not only tells us what happened, but it makes us feel. It creates empathy for what our ancestors went through in difficult times. Since human nature never changes, historical fiction helps us make sense of the current world. What lies in people's hearts is still the same. We are not so far from ancient people as we may think. As President Harry S. Truman once said, "There is nothing new in the world except the history you do not know."[1]

Learning the truth of history is important, even if you don't like what you learn. In fact, it takes great effort to seek the truth and not be guided by negative emotions or prejudices. As Elvis Presley is widely noted to have said, "Truth is like the sun. You can shut it out

---

1. "Harry S. Truman Quotes," *Truman State University*, https://www.truman.edu/about/history/our-namesake/truman-quotes/.

for a time, but it ain't goin' away."[2] However truth is viewed, truth gives us freedom, and many of us spend our entire lives searching for it. Our desire for truth gives us the deep hunger to answer questions such as "Why am I here?" Because truth will never change, there is only one answer to these questions. Many of us have heard that the truth will set you free, and we could certainly apply those words to academia. However, the original intent of those words comes from a passage in the Bible in John 8 that discusses a spiritual freedom from the bondage of sin.

This book will share the famous Bible story about a Roman centurion's faith. Healing the centurion's servant is one of Jesus's miracles told in the Gospels of Matthew and Luke. According to these accounts, a Roman centurion asks Jesus for help because his servant is desperately ill. Jesus offers to go to the centurion's home to perform a healing, but the centurion believes that Jesus's word of authority will be sufficient. Jesus is impressed by the faith of this man who happens to be a Gentile. He grants the help and heals the servant that same day.

Since the true back story of the centurion is unknown, we have to use our imaginations to create a story for this extraordinary man. In this book, our journey starts with the Great Roman Civil War (49–55 BC) that ultimately ended with Caesar in full control of Rome, and then it visits the conflict between Mark Antony and Octavian. You will learn what life was like in the Roman Army, and you will also experience how the ordinary people of the time lived. You will meet many historic characters—Caesar, Mark Antony, Cleopatra, Octavian, and Herod—and religious figures of the day, most notably Rabbi Hillel and Rabbi Shammai. In short, you will learn how it was to live in the first century during the time of Jesus.

---

2. "Elvis Presley Quotes," *Brainy Quotes*, https://www.brainyquote.com/quotes/elvis_presley_133068.

INTRODUCTION

The final blow to the enemies of Gaius Julius Caesar during the bloody Roman Civil War started with the death of Gnaeus Pompeius Magnus (Pompey the Great), a famous military commander. In 60 BC, Pompey joined with rivals Julius Caesar and Marcus Licinius Crassus to form the First Triumvirate, and together, the trio ruled Rome for seven years. Pompey would even go on to marry Caesar's daughter, Julia. But the death of Julia during childbirth took the last restraint off Pompey, and his jealousy of Caesar's successes led him to collapse the political alliance in 53 BC. The Roman Senate supported Pompey and asked Caesar to step down from his army. Caesar flatly refused to give up his veteran legions and instead crossed the Rubicon River from Cisalpine Gaul into Italy, where he muttered the famous words, "Let the die be cast," or "Let the dice fly high." Crossing the Rubicon River, Caesar began a civil war. He had early victories in Italy and Spain but was later routed and forced to flee to Greece. In August 48 BC, with a smaller army than Pompey, Caesar turned the tides of defeat into victory. A humiliated Pompey, completely bested by Caesar, fled to Egypt.

Pompey hoped the Egyptian king Ptolemy, whom he had previously supported, would return the favor and help him. Ptolemy was only 13 years old at the time, and his counselors advised him that friendship with the powerful Caesar was more important than old ties to a vanquished man who had no army. Pompey was waiting for Ptolemy's answer in a ship offshore. The answer came in the form of two veterans who had fought beside Pompey in his legions years ago but were now serving the Egyptian government. On September 28, 48 BC, Pompey was invited to leave his ship and come ashore at Pelusium. The veterans warmly invited him ashore to meet with the pharaoh. They rowed out in a small boat and away from Pompey's ship, deceiving Pompey and stabbing him in the back. In front of his wife and children, who were on the ship from which he had just disembarked, they cut off his head, stripped his body, and took his head to the pharaoh, insultingly leaving the body naked and unattended on shore. Fortunately, one of his servants managed to gather some timber and cremated his body there.

Caesar later visited Ptolemy and, when presented with the head of his old friend and enemy, turned away from Ptolemy with loathing. Ptolemy gave him Pompey's signet ring on which was engraved a lion holding a sword in his paws, prompting Caesar to burst into tears. Ptolemy's advisers had completely misjudged the Roman sense of honor. Caesar demanded the assassins be executed and had Pompey's head sent to his family to be cremated with honor. Ptolemy was later deposed in favor of his sister, Cleopatra.

With Pompey defeated, the war continued for a short time since Caesar had a few months of cleanup work against the remaining senatorial forces in Africa left. After several minor battles, the senatorial forces finally lined up for a major battle near Thapsus under Scipio, Caesar's former comrade. Caesar's mostly veteran army held unquestionable loyalty to him, while senatorial forces lacked heart, with some switching sides because of Caesar's legendary ability. His now-famous clemency toward fellow Romans played a part as well. Caesar easily routed his enemies, and many surrendered, but 10,000 men had no such luck, fleeing to a nearby hill as Caesar's enraged army pursued them. Perhaps the show of cowardice, along with the frustration of months of being refused a major battle, was too much for Caesar's men to restrain themselves. His veterans slaughtered them all. The leaders of the senatorial forces were defeated. Cato, one of the senatorial leaders, retired to his private chamber and fell on his own sword rather than bow down to Caesar. A disappointed Caesar, who had hoped to bring a defeated and pardoned Cato back to Rome, later reportedly said, "Cato, I must grudge you your death, as you grudged me the honor of saving your life."[1] Caesar, age 54, added the conquest of Africa to his list of accomplishments and sailed back to Rome.

---

1. Plutarch, *Plutarch's Lives of Illustrious Men, Volume 2* (New York: John B. Alden Publisher, 1887), 543, Google Books.

CHAPTER I
CIVIL WAR

SPQR

In Rome, Liborius, an inauspicious slave taken from Gaul, was waiting impatiently for his master to return with a triumphant Caesar. Gaul had become a large province of the Roman Empire after Caesar defeated it in the Gallic Wars between 58 and 51 BC. The Gauls were originally Celtic people but lost their tribal identities after the Roman Conquest. Nearly one in five of the population across the Roman Empire were slaves, and upon this foundation, the Roman state and society were built. Most Roman slaves were war captives who were sold quickly after being taken in order to avoid the cost of feeding and guarding them in a hostile country.

Liborius remembered very little of his childhood, only feeling discomfort when he thought of his youth. Almost since he was old enough to walk, he had run loose in the forest. The mighty trees clothed in green sheltered every kind of life and blocked most of the blue sky. He remembered the air, rich with fragrance after a rainfall, the smell of the earth, and the cool watered ponds and streams where he had learned to swim. His blue eyes were a river full of life. His dark brown curls with reddish highlights lent him an untamed look.

5

When he was a child, play was his priority, and he would dodge and run past rotting trees and under low branches, climbing the moss-covered stones. He barely remembered his mother, as she had died from an unknown illness when he was very young. His father, brother of the tribal leader, had not yet remarried and did his best to raise him but was often gone to raid other tribes. Liborius was raised mostly by relatives in the tribe, who worked to tame his wild nature.

Then war came to his tribe, the Nervii, from the Romans. Until their defeat, the Nervians were one of the most powerful Celtic tribes of northern Gaul. His father and all the able-bodied men went to war against the invaders. Liborius, a child of only 10 years old, stayed behind with the women, children, and elderly of his kinfolk. The men did not return. The Nervii warriors fought hard, standing on the bodies of slain comrades and shouting in defiance at the Romans, proudly fighting to the last man. Caesar thought the tribe was punished enough, and the Nervii would be one of the few to gain Caesar's mercy. He developed a high opinion of the Nervians who had shown great fighting spirit in carrying out such a vigorous attack, even when the tide of battle turned irretrievably against them. The men and warriors would see death, but most of the tribe would be spared, and the surrounding tribes were warned not to take advantage of their weakness. The women wept as Caesar's victorious legion came upon them after their victory, and the children were quickly separated from their mothers. A small number, approximately 100, were hand-picked and taken as spoils. Liborius was among this group of children, but he held no resentment for the Romans. To the victor go the spoils. A legionnaire named Lucius of the Tenth Legion received Liborius as a reward.

Lucius was famous for heroism with the Tenth Legion in the Battle of the Sabis, or the battle against the Nervians in 57 BC. During the battle against the Nervians, the Ninth Legion, together with the Tenth Legion, defeated the tribe of the Atrebates and then moved against the tribes of northern Gaul on the other side of a river and captured the enemy camp. From that position, the Tenth could see how desperate the situation was for the Twelfth and the Seventh Legions against the Nervii, so they quickly charged downhill, crossed the river, and attacked the Nervians from the rear, trapping them and giving them little hope of survival. Lucius led the desperate charge downhill. This was not the first time Lucius displayed such fearlessness; he previously displayed courage when he was the aquilifer of the Tenth Legion. An aquilifer was a senior veteran who was given the honor of bearing the Eagle Standard of a Roman legion. Some time ago when the landing invasion of Briton was not going well, Lucius threw himself overboard and, carrying the Eagle Standard, advanced alone against the enemy. His comrades, fearing disgrace, with one accord leapt down from the ship and were followed by the remaining troops from the other ships. Lucius was rewarded for his bravery in Briton by a promotion to optio, second in command to a centurion.

For his heroism against the Nervians, Lucius was promoted from optio to a full centurion of the mighty Tenth and given full Roman citizenship along with Liborius as a gift. At the time, the promotion was the more valuable of the gifts to Lucius. A centurion was an officer of the Roman Army in charge of 80 to 100 soldiers. A legion may have been led by a general or a legate, the overall legion commander, but the legion's day-to-day operations and discipline in battle were led by the centurion.

Before joining the army, Lucius had been a simple olive farmer from the Roman province of Baetica. This territory was one of three provinces in Hispania, modern-day Spain, that sat at the bottom of southern Hispania near the fabled Pillars of Hercules. Roman possession of Hispania began after the defeat of Carthage in the Second Punic War. Before Romanization, the mountainous area that was to become Baetica was occupied by several settled Iberian tribal groups. Celtic influence was there but not as strong as it was in Gaul. Baetica was agriculturally rich, providing wine exports, olive oil, and fermented fish sauce called garum, all staples of the Mediterranean diet. Lucius was a poor farmer from modest means with no heredity title, and he thought joining the Roman Army was a good move. Lucius with his big, expressive round eyes, chestnut colored hair, and a well-muscled build would make the ideal Roman soldier. There were many benefits of joining the Roman Army. First, it was a great career. Soldiers could receive an annual salary paid in denarii. Non-citizen soldiers, called auxiliaries, were awarded Roman citizenship at the end of 25 years. After 20 to 25 years of service, soldiers typically had their choice of land or a lump sum in denarii. If they were not already Roman citizens, they received citizenship for their service. Some men joined for the glory—they knew how important it was to defend the world's most powerful city—but most joined for the coins in their pockets. Soldiers were respected by all Roman citizens. Ladies swooned over them. If they survived, there was always a chance for promotion. To be promoted, they needed to be one of the best. With promotion came rewards, and they would be exempt from many of the duties of an ordinary soldier and would be paid more denarii.

Liborius traveled with the Tenth Legion, serving his master Lucius who lived and worked at camp. The marching camp was built every day to a standard plan with food and sanitation in design. Typically, Roman soldiers lived in healthy conditions even on the march. Liborius tended to his master, preparing food available from the supply. An important duty was to keep Lucius' sword sharpened and maintain his uniform, particularly his sandals. The master's power over the slave, called *dominica potestas*, was absolute. A master had complete control over a slave. It was his right to torture, humiliate, and even kill a slave. In the eyes of the law, slaves had no property rights and could not marry. Whatever the power over slaves, Roman masters, although not known as compassionate people, understood the value of their slave property. Most slaves were treated fairly, but ultimately, it was up to their individual masters. Liborius was lucky, for he was treated fairly by Lucius. Other slaves who served the legion were not as fortunate. Lucius was a grizzled warrior who demanded the highest standards, but as long as duties were performed to his specifications, he was not harsh. Liborius lived a tough life on the campaign working alongside soldiers as they disassembled camps to move or dug trenches when needed. Some of the soldiers even spoke to Liborius perhaps to share news of a battle or camp gossip.

The Tenth Legion was created when a much younger Caesar arrived as governor in the province of Baetica, or Hispania Ulterior. In 61 BC, he quickly decided to subdue the west and northwest areas, now modern-day Portugal. He already had two legions based in the province. They were the Eighth and Ninth Legions, which had been enlisted in 65 BC. Caesar needed a third legion for his planned campaign and so immediately enlisted a new legion. The Tenth Legion was the first legion levied personally by Caesar and was consistently his most trusted.

The Tenth would go down in history as the most celebrated Roman legion. Its exploits began with the Gallic campaigns, which brought the Tenth Legion from Spain along with the Seventh, Eighth, and Ninth Legions. Almost immediately, the Tenth was put into action. In the summer of 58 BC, the Tenth Legion fought in major actions, including the battles of Arar and Bibracte against the Helvetii tribes. The defeat of the Helvetii tribes prevented their migration from present-day Switzerland to western France.

The Tenth Legion received the famed nickname Equestris (mounted) after an incident just after the defeat of the Helvetii. The leaders of the Gallic tribes petitioned Caesar for aid against their enemy at a peace conference but insisted that each side should only be accompanied by mounted troops. They made this a condition, knowing that Caesar's cavalry was composed mainly of Gallic auxiliaries whose loyalty to Caesar was questionable. Caesar was not a fool and ordered the auxiliaries to dismount. He had legionnaires from the Tenth ride in their place to accompany him to the peace conference.

After Caesar's military victories that expanded the Roman Empire, a jealous Roman Senate demanded he surrender his army. Caesar refused and the Tenth Legion chose to follow Caesar across the shallow Rubicon River. The Tenth would uphold Caesar's glory and went to destroy the senatorial forces. Liborius was separated from his master for the first time since he had been given to Lucius. Liborius was to wait in Rome and care for his master's home while Lucius traveled with the Tenth, defending Caesar's honor. Lucius finally had a chance to spend some coins and purchased a modest, one-floor flat in Rome.

Liborius was disappointed that he was not allowed to follow his master with the Tenth. Although he faked a great smile for Lucius as the warrior departed, his heart was broken. He thought, *Would not I be more valuable to my master than caring for his new home?* All-consuming military life was more preferred than a dull life tending a home. For Liborius, military life with its constant interaction and labor was replaced with occasional visits to purchase food at the market and hoping for a knock at the door. He also could not escape to the blessings of nature where he felt most alive. Without his previous life with the army, Liborius was restless like the wind. Dealing with the grip of boredom and loneliness would be his hardest task. Every night, he stared at the moon's silver glow, wishing his life would change.

CHAPTER II

WHEN IN ROME,
LIVE AS THEY DO

SPQR

The sun began to rise over Rome, first touching the tall stone buildings, a symbol of Rome's endurance and strength. It was early morning, and no crowds headed to the bread doles or to entertainment. No children were chasing through the narrow streets. Over a million inhabitants would wake soon to labor, relax, or eat.

Rome was a melting pot that included Greeks, Syrians, Jews, North Africans, Spaniards, Gauls, and Britons. While their daily lives could often be hard, citizens always survived because of the grain dole given to everyone who was willing to stand in line for their allotment once a month at one of the public granaries. Outside the city walls, in the nearby towns and on small farms, people lived a simpler life. The rural areas were more dependent on the fruits of their own labor. City dwellers, however, had more routine in their lives, going about various trades available to them such as banking, carpentry, or fishing. Slaves in the city performed all the menial jobs for doctors, teachers, and barbers. The rural people flocked to the city with the promises of jobs and a better way of life, but in reality, city life fulfilled few of these promises. Many of these dreamers now lived in the poorer parts of the city, and countless were homeless. Only free-born Roman men were allowed to wear togas as a sign of Roman citizenship, while Roman women wore stolas. Liborius, like most slaves, wore a simple, knee-length tunic called a chilton.

Lucius was fortunate that his home was not an apartment like many of the poor in the city. Life in these apartment buildings was not pleasant. Sunlight was lacking in these cramped quarters, and the buildings were boiling in the summer and freezing in the winter. When the people did not have access to communal toilets with a shared sponge for wiping, they dumped human waste onto the streets. Besides a foul stench, this led to a breeding ground for illness and disease. The fear of fire in these decaying buildings was always a constant reality.

Liborius was spending his time cleaning the flat, washing clothes, and tending a small garden. Occasionally, Liborius heard news about the Civil War. He was concerned to hear about the Battle of Dyrrhachium near Greece. When news came, it was not good. During that battle, Caesar, fearing that the Tenth Legion would be outflanked by reinforcements led by Pompey, had ordered them to retreat. The rest of Caesar's army, seeing the mighty Tenth retreating for the first time, broke and fled to their camps. The Tenth, seeing the army routed, also fled. After the embarrassing defeat, the Tenth demanded to be decimated for cowardice. Decimation was a punishment that fell by lot. All men were eligible for execution, regardless of the individual's degree of fault or their rank. It was common in a mutiny to rig the lot in order to eliminate the mutiny ringleaders. Since it could not be rigged and because of Caesar's love for the Tenth, he was reluctant and demoted the Tenth Legion's standard bearers instead. Liborius was pleased to learn that his master was spared from decimation and injury from battle.

For four long years, Liborius waited for his master's return. His life was quite boring compared to life with the Tenth. He would often dream about life on campaign with the Tenth and one day joining them as a legionnaire after first earning his freedom. How he would earn his freedom was uncertain. He somehow needed to save money with permission and use it to buy freedom for a sum his master set. He doubted Lucius would prevent him from saving the money. Lifelong obedience and services (*obsequium et operae*) toward the former owner would be part of his freedom, although he would have the right to trade and make his own living.

In one dream, Liborius watched the barbarian hordes in front of the Tenth about 500 feet slightly uphill just outside thick woods. They were in a frenzy, banging their swords on their shields. That these barbarians sought individual glory would be their downfall. The Legion marched as one. In this dream, Liborius held the standard of the Tenth Legion high in the front ranks. Arrows filled the sky and dropped off the legionnaires' shields as the barbarians fired on them futilely. The Tenth launched heavy spears and darts to break down the opposing formation, and then the barbarians charged. The legionnaires formed together tightly and drew their gladiuses. They would use these short swords to thrust between shields and attempt to gut the torsos of the enemy. They could also use the swords in a hacking motion to hack off limbs and slice at an opponent's legs beneath his shield if that was the only opening. The barbarian hordes hit hard, and the line began to falter. In flew Caesar to the front lines at the critical moment. The Tenth was inspired by their commander, pressing the attack. Their fighting technique was not fancy with individual heroics as was the barbarians' style. The Legion fought together as methodical killing machines. The new recruits fought in front, and the veterans fought in the rear. As the front ranks tired, they rotated new men to replace them. The legions fought up the hill even though the enemy was on good ground. It was a mass of blood and guts. The Gauls fought heroically and didn't stop, although the bodies of their comrades lay everywhere. It ended quickly as a massacre. Typically in ancient warfare, once a victor is determined, woe to the other side because chaos quickly turns to slaughter. A cheer rang out—Roma Victor!—and the Tenth celebrated victory. Roman citizens heard news that the brutal Civil War was finally over and the great Caesar was returning triumphantly. A nervous energy gripped Rome with the people fearing what a triumphant Caesar would look like. It was late at night when the long, overdue Lucius returned from the exhausting campaign. A worn-out Lucius said not a word as he entered his home and collapsed on his bed. Liborius was excited to hear stories of the Tenth but did not dare disturb his weary master.

It was late morning when Lucius finally awoke and dragged himself out of bed. Liborius attended him and prepared a large meal of bread with dates and honey. Lucius was hungry and ate heartily. Liborius set his heart on knowing about Lucius's adventures but waited for Lucius to talk. Lucius could see the glint in Liborius's eye. With a smile, Lucius told of the battles and the campaigns of the Tenth. He finished by telling Liborius in a proud voice that shortly, the Tenth Legion would be marching with Caesar in a quadruple triumph.

The end of four wars was to be celebrated. The war in Gaul is where Caesar had brought many large tribes under Roman control and subdued others that had rebelled.

The war against Pharnances of Pontus was evidently so swift and complete that Caesar spoke his famous words, *Veni, vidi, vici* (I came, I saw, I conquered). Then there was the African war against King Juba who had supported Scipio. There was the Egyptian war in which he could have annexed Egypt but instead restored Cleopatra to her throne as queen. A triumph was held to publicly celebrate and sanctify the success of a military commander who had led his forces to victory. Caesar's triumphs had long been denied. He had been at war for many years, and at his first chance, due to victories against native tribes in the Roman province of Hispania Ulterior, he sacrificed his triumphant to be elected to his first consulship. Liborius would be allowed to see the triumph, and he eagerly awaited it.

Liborius worked hard daily polishing Lucius's armor, which was much needed after a long military campaign. The heavy-soled, hobnailed sandals, called Caligae, worn by Lucius, needed to be replaced. Wasting no time, Liborius took them to a busy craftsman in Rome. Patiently, he waited as the craftsman placed the sandals on an iron block and then hammered in the iron nails. Bringing them home, he further prepared them by first backing them with a solution called melanteria and then waterproofing them with an application of grease. The morning of the triumph parade, the uniform was ready. Lucius, his hand laid kindly upon Liborius's shoulder, told his servant to enjoy the parade. Lucius then departed his home with feverish excitement. Liborius gazed upon Lucius as he departed. Lucius looked like a powerful figure in armor. On his head was a brazen helmet, and on his body was a shining, newly polished breastplate and skirt of mail; and don't forget his new, black caligae sandals. Liborius departed shortly after Lucius to find a place to watch the triumph, which, truth be told, could be the greatest Roman triumph ever witnessed.

CHAPTER III
CAESAR'S TRIUMPH

L iborius, wearing a woolen, brown tunic, stood in the crowd watching Caesar's triumph. Caesar, under the gaze of his peers and an applauding crowd, was making his way to the Temple of Jupiter, the most important temple in ancient Rome, located on the Capitoline Hill. In Republican Rome, truly exceptional military achievement merited the highest possible honors, which connected the Roman triumph with a civil ceremony and religious rites of ancient Rome. They were held to publicly celebrate and sanctify the success of a military commander who had led Roman forces to victory in the service of the state or, originally and traditionally, one who had successfully completed a foreign war. This was the first of four celebrated triumphs, four in a single month but at intervals of a few days.

Caesar rode in the procession, drawn through the city in a four-horse chariot. The bright, white horses were truly magnificent. From earlier times, the rare white horse had been mythologized as possessing exceptional divination. Caesar wore the purple and gold regalia, traditionally associated both with the ancient Roman monarchy and the Capitoline Temple. He also wore a laurel crown and red boots but chose not to don the red-painted face of Rome's supreme deity. Music from tubas and pipes could barely be heard over the crowd's roar. All this was done to the strewing of flowers and clouds of incense. The auriga, a slave with gladiator status, drove the chariot and had an extra job of whispering periodically to a triumphant commander so he would remember that he was only a man.

The triumphant moved in a fairly standard processional order. First came the captive leaders and soldiers walking in chains. Later, the leaders would be executed or further displayed. They carted their captured weapons, armor, gold, silver, statuary, and curious or exotic treasures behind them. The treasure and money, valued at 65,000 talents and paraded in triumphal processions, was said to weigh 20,414 pounds. Several floats followed with 20 pictures showing all the events and persons involved, except for Pompey who alone decided not to be portrayed since he was still much missed by all. The crowd laughed at the rout of enemies but groaned at the disasters for their own people in the Civil War, particularly when they saw Scipio stabbing himself in the chest.

A notable appearance was Cleopatra holding her son, Caesarion. Cleopatra was a member of the Ptolemaic dynasty, a Greek family of Macedonian origin that ruled Egypt after Alexander the Great's death during the Hellenistic Period. The Ptolemies spoke Greek throughout their dynasty and refused to speak Egyptian. By contrast, Cleopatra learned to speak Egyptian and represented herself as the reincarnation of the Egyptian goddess Isis. She walked with Ptolemy XIV, her younger brother and co-regent. Ptolemy XIV, not to be confused with the Ptolemy who had angered Caesar. Ptolemy XIV was a puppet ruler, with Cleopatra holding the real power. Cleopatra was 21 years old and not as breathtaking as rumored. She was shorter than the women of Rome and had a prominent nose. She first met Caesar by slipping past the guards of Ptolemy XIV, rolled up in a carpet. This audacity impressed Caesar who was 52 at the time. She looked men in the eye when she spoke and possessed a razor-sharp wit and keen intellect. He loved her personality rather than her looks, which he found deficient. They became lovers during Caesar's stay in Egypt, and she gave birth to their son Ptolemy Caesar in 47 BC, nine months after their first meeting. The love child was nicknamed Caesarion, which means "little Caesar." Cleopatra claimed publicly that Caesar was the father of her son and wished him to name the boy his heir, but Caesar refused, choosing his grandnephew Octavian instead. The relationship between Cleopatra and Caesar was obvious to the Roman people, and the majority did not approve.

Next in line, all on foot, came Rome's senators and magistrates, followed by the general's lictors in their red war robes, their fasces wreathed in laurel. Lictors, who were members of an ancient Roman class of magisterial attendants, carried the fasces, the symbols of power, for their magistrate and were constantly in his attendance in public. They cleared his way in crowds and summoned and punished his offenders. After the lictors rode Caesar in his four-horse chariot. His unarmed soldiers followed in togas and laurel crowns, chanting *io triumphe* and singing bawdy songs at their general's expense.

The procession came to its ending point at the Capitoline Temple. This grand temple served as the center for the official religion of Rome and was surrounded by the Capitulina precinct, which included a number of statues, shrines, and altars to the Roman gods. Two flawless white oxen were led for the sacrifice to Jupiter, garland-decked and with gilded horns, along with tokens of his victory to be laid at Jupiter's feet. Officially, Caesar dedicated his victory to the Roman Senate, people, and gods. After the triumph, the people departed, even more curious as to what the returned Caesar would do next.

Liborius enjoyed the triumph parade. Watching the spectacle reinforced his desire to one day join the Roman Army and end his boring life. He applauded and cheered until his voice was hoarse when the Tenth Legion marched by. After the parade, he worked his way through the crowds toward home. It wasn't easy since people had poured in from all over the countryside to get a glimpse of the extravaganza in the already crowded city. He navigated the narrow alleyways and labyrinth of lanes and passageways, quietly hoping a chamber pot or excrement would not crash on his head. He also looked out for shadowy figures. No police protected crime victims in Rome; it was a matter of self-help. Liborius quickened his pace before darkness came, wishing he was armed.

He made it back to the simple flat Lucius owned. He quickly prepared dinner and then waited for Lucius to return home. After a long wait, it was evident that Lucius would not be coming back for dinner. Lucius and the veterans did have a lot to celebrate. Years of constant war were finally over. There was plenty to celebrate. Liborius ate and then cleaned up the dinner mess. Exhausted from the day, he went to bed and slept soundly.

Immediately after the last triumph, Caesar gave out gifts, exceeding all his promises to his veteran soldiers. He gave 5,000 denarii to each soldier, and centurions received double that amount. To each military officer, double again, and amazingly to each member of the plebs, or common people, 100 denarii. Most of the veterans grumbled at the gift to the plebs, thinking it should have all been given to them. In addition to the distributions of spoils, Caesar put on various shows. There were horse races, musical contests, and gladiatorial combats. During previously unheard of gladiatorial matches, a thousand foot soldiers opposed another thousand, another had 200 cavalry on each side, and another was mixed infantry with cavalry combat. There was also a naval battle with 4,000 oarsmen and 1,000 marines on each side to fight.

Caesar also spent lavishly and had the Temple of Venus Genetrix built. He had publicly proclaimed his ancestry to the goddess Venus throughout his life. He believed the goddess protected him against Pompey and vowed to build a shrine to Venus in appreciation for her support. Around the temple, he laid out a district that he made into a square for the Romans, not a market square but a place where people could meet to settle business, similar to that of the Persians who also had a square for those who wanted to obtain or learn about justice. Unquestioned, he even erected a beautiful, golden statue of Cleopatra, represented as Isis in the Temple of Venus Genetrix.

The Egyptian queen, Cleopatra, settled into one of Caesar's country houses just outside Rome. As a foreign head of state, she was not allowed inside Rome's pomerium. The pomerium was a religious open space just inside the walls of the early city in Rome, and everything beyond it was simply territory belonging to Rome. The relationship between Cleopatra and Caesar was obvious to the Roman people and caused a scandal because Caesar was already married to Calpurnia. A foreign mistress or a fling with a slave was acceptable, and as a Roman elite, Caesar could have all the affairs he wanted, with men or with women of any class, as long as he was the initiating partner. The scandal and anger was that Roman society was ruled by a male oligarchy. To maintain their power, the Roman elite needed clear lines of inheritance. There could never be any confusion about who fathered a baby.

Lucius eventually reappeared after the triumph's conclusion. He was not home much in the beginning, spending a lot of time enjoying the extravagant festivities that concluded with long nights drinking with his brothers-in-arms and flirting with the barmaids. There was also fun to be had in the clubs and gambling locations in the city. Liborius, unable to join his master in the revelry, stayed behind with the boring tasks of tending to Lucius's home. His life there was reduced to minute details and relentless routine.

The very last day of the festivities, Lucius appeared at the door early in the morning, as if he had just seen a free spirit released by Pluto, the Roman god of the dead and underworld.

"Liborius," his tongue stuttered, "it's over. It's the end. The soldiers of the Tenth Legion are to be disbanded. They are to be given land to settle in Narbonne, southern Gaul, and to populate the next generation of legionnaires." Calming himself with an effort, he continued. "It looks like retirement for me . . . time to finally put my armor away." Liborius was at a loss for words as the knowledge sank in: *I'm going to be forever a house slave.*

Lucius continued. "Some loyal veterans along with Caesar supporters will be given positions in the new government, including some in the Senate. Caesar himself sent a message for me to visit with him tomorrow at his home." Lucius smiled. "To see Caesar, what an honor, what a privilege."

Liborius suppressed a frown of disappointment on his face and made his best attempt to smile back. Lucius's stay was short, and he returned to the entertainment in Rome. Late at night, Liborius helped drag his master to bed and then went off to bed himself. It was hard to sleep. Traveling with the Tenth Legion had truly been more enjoyable than his life now. He began to catch glimpses of life and routine that was as relentless as death.

The next day, Liborius helped his master dress in his toga after giving him a scraping for the big day. While Romans liked to keep clean, they did not use soap. Instead, they applied perfumed oils to their skin and then scraped it off with a tool known as a strigil. Liborius was excited to hear he would accompany Lucius to Caesar's villa. Lucius was still recovering from last night's debauchery and wanted a companion for the long walk. They took nothing for the trip with the exception of Lucius's gladius because they never knew what could happen on the road.

They walked along the well-constructed viae early in the morning. The Roman viaes differed from the many other smaller or rougher dirt roads, bridle paths, and tracks. To make these roads, the Romans used stones—broken stones mixed with cement and sand—so the water could drain, and on top they used tightly packed paving stones. The Roman road networks were important both for maintaining the stability of the empire and for its expansion. The legions had a good time on them as did Lucius and Liborius on the trip to Caesar's villa.

Caesar lived in the ancestral home of his first and most beloved wife, Cornelia, just outside Rome. The villa was common, a one-floor home built around a large courtyard known as an atrium. These atria were exposed to the weather and had various-sized rooms off them. A beloved room that was attached was the peristylium. This popular meeting area was loved for its comfort and being shaded from the rough sun. It boasted the beauty of nature with a charming garden. To visit Caesar's home was an unbelievable accolade, and both Liborius and Lucius were ecstatic. In silence, the men walked, setting a good pace.

It was late afternoon when they arrived. A servant met them at the door and guided them through the adjoining vestibule where they removed their cloaks to be stored until the return trip. The slave then washed the guests' feet since the streets were dusty and full of animal droppings. They were escorted through the main rooms decorated with colored plaster walls and beautiful mosaic floors. The villa was nothing like the flat that Liborius lived in with Lucius. The images on the decorated floors were amazing. They depicted animals and scenes, the most notable of which was Alexander the Great in a battle against the Persians. The image of Alexander was so lifelike that it appeared to spring out from the floor. They could hear the water flow from the pipes throughout the villa. Unlike flats and apartments, the villa held more comforts. Aqueducts fed lead pipes that brought water to the house for many uses, including the hypocaust that heated the under-floor and kept baths hot. Lucius and Liborius passed furniture that was very basic and practical as well as some stools and a few reclining couches. They entered the peristylium, a garden surrounded by columns that supported a shady, roofed portico that had inner walls embellished with elaborate wall paintings. A beautiful statue of Vesta, the goddess of the home, was prominently displayed.

A servant motioned for Liborius to follow him, and Lucius stood in the garden waiting for Caesar to arrive. Liborius was led to a stool in a room used for storage just outside the peristylium to wait for his master's return. Once the fellow slave left the room, a temptation struck Liborius to catch a closer glimpse of Caesar and hear the conversation in the peristylium. The temptation quickly faded. As rumored, Caesar was so strict in the management of his household, in small matters as well as in those of greater importance, that he put his baker in irons for serving him one kind of bread and his guests another. Having not the courage to sneak a peek, Liborius decided to listen instead, and he moved closer to the entrance of the room. When he thought he was at a safe distance, he waited. It felt like an eternity in those few minutes until he heard Caesar.

Caesar appeared before Lucius. Caesar was tall with a fair complexion. His body appeared lean and physically fit. His face held piercing black eyes that appeared to look through you. "Lucius, I heard you bought a home in Rome. Many years ago, when I was a young man, this villa was taken from me during the persecutions of the Roman Consul Sulla when I was stripped of my inheritance for refusing to divorce my wife, Cornelia. After the persecutions and with the help of her parents, I received it back. After being so long away, it is truly good to be home." Caesar sighed. "My Rome has changed, but I will always love her. I stood up for Roman spirit then, and I stand up for Roman spirit and values now."

"You have always been a good patron of spreading Roman culture," answered Lucius.

In a matter-of-fact voice, Caesar replied, "We conquered because we could. The conquered of Rome fought for freedom, such as I would have done in their situation. We conquered not to spread our culture but because we could. The world is changing. This is a new world we live in, and the rulers of it have an army backing them. Though the armies of my enemies are defeated, there is still a fight, and I need loyal followers to fill vacant positions in Rome. I offer you a position as senator if you will have it."

Lucius thought for a short moment and then spoke. "I am a soldier, my dear Caesar, not a politician. The life of a legionnaire is all

I know. Unless the Tenth is called up again, I will retire to my home in Rome, find a wife, raise a family, and produce sons to join the army. I appreciate your offer and I am honored, but I must decline."

Caesar nodded, filled two chalices of calda, and handed one to Lucius. This wine was a mixture of warm water, wine, and spices. Caesar sighed, "I respect your wishes, Lucius, and appreciate your service and loyalty. The army helped me get to my current position, and I will never forget that. Now go and have those sons, Lucius, and a long life to you."

Caesar needed to depart for business but bade Lucius to have some dinner before he left. Not wanting to offend his host, Lucius decided to stay and eat. He had Liborius join him for a meal located at the center of the house near the hearth. A small statue of Vesta, the goddess of the hearth and home, stood close by. She was known as a quiet, well-behaved goddess who didn't join in the arguments and fights of the other deities. One of Caesar's servants brought them each a plate of beans, onions, and peas that were cooked in an earthenware pot hanging over a fire and rendered a little more interesting by the addition of game meat. They were given garum, a distinctive fish sauce, to add flavor to the dish. For dessert, they ate dried pears, figs, and oysters. They also drank plenty of wine. At the conclusion of the meal, as was the tradition in most Roman homes, a small cake was thrown on the fire for Vesta. It was considered good luck as it burned with a crackle.

After eating, Liborius and Lucius headed back to Rome, moving at a brisk pace along the country road. Unfortunately, they would be returning to Rome in the dark. Many of the city's residents avoided the streets of Rome after dark. The vigils provided the only public protection, but their primary duty at night was to look out for fire, a frequent occurrence in Rome. The biggest fear at night was muggers. Aware of the threat, Liborius and Lucius knew to tread cautiously into the city. Lucius had his hands on the hilt of his sword, ready for anything.

They entered the gates of Rome with no problem and headed to the first floor flat they now called home. They moved at a quick pace, watching out for threats. In a darker part of the city, a solitary figure appeared from the shadows holding a small dagger in a feeble attempt to rob them. Lucius motioned for Liborius to get behind him. Lucius, the veteran of many battles, quickly drew his gladius and waited. The thief froze and stared at the gladius. He had expected easy prey, not a stone-faced Roman soldier. It did not take long for Lucius to examine the situation. In no time, the grizzled veteran could not control himself and roared with laughter, helpless and doubled over. The laughter was contagious. Liborius joined him with tears rolling down his cheeks. The two of them howled until their stomach muscles were sore and then tapered off to exaggerated sighs. The mugger stood in shock for a moment and then ran off in fear. Liborius and Lucius sniffled the remaining way home.

CHAPTER IV
CAESAR'S DOWNFALL

Julius Caesar sat on the stone steps outside the entrance of his villa. Physically and mentally, the proud defender of Rome was exhausted, and his face looked like it. Ambition still filled his veins, and he dreamed of future campaigns, but for now, he would relax. His wife, Calpurnia, approached him and sat down next to him. Calpurnia poked his arm lightly.

"Tired?" She smiled, folding her hands in her lap.

"I'm fine," he muttered. His eyes settled on her. "It is good to be home after all these years, good to be alive, unharmed from battle, and free to finally do for Rome what I have so long dreamed about."

She sighed gently. "You cannot conquer all your dreams in one day. Let us at least enjoy today. I missed you, my husband." She lightly touched him on the shoulder then kissed him on the cheek.

Caesar did not relax long, and in time, his attempt to usurp more power from the Roman Republic made even his long-time admirers pause. In early 44 BC, Caesar was given the title dictator for life. Rumors persisted that Caesar wanted to be made king. It did not work out well for the last Roman king. Tarquinius Superbus, the last king of Rome, was removed in a revolution that led to Rome being governed as a republic. In a version of democracy, for it was often a rigged process, two top leaders of the Roman Republic were elected consuls by the people. This prevented any one ruler from becoming a tyrant. After the compliant Senate declared that upon his death Caesar would become an official god of the Roman state, there was a perception that Caesar had become too power-mad for comfort. Several unpopular events followed, including Caesar mocking the senators even after they'd voted him honors before the Temple of Venus Genetrix, refusing to rise for them. Finally, one episode was seen by many as the final straw.

On February 15, most Romans took part in the annual Lupercalia fertility festival. The festival, observed in the city of Rome, was to prevent evil spirits and purify the city, and also to release health and fertility. At the end of the festival and after a sacrifice, priests wearing only loincloths ran around and touched bystanders with goatskin straps to bless their fertility. At the pinnacle of the festival, Caesar sat atop the speaker's platform in the Roman Forum that was used to address the people. Mark Antony, one of Caesar's trusted lieutenants and chief priest of Rome, climbed the platform and, with a frozen audience, placed the crown on Caesar's head, proclaiming that the people wanted Caesar to have it. Caesar removed the crown after another offer and cried out to the crowd, "Only Jupiter is king of the gods and the Romans!" Perhaps Caesar did not want to be king, or perhaps he was checking the mood of the people, but this was a turning point for those who wanted him dead.

Three main players wanted Caesar lifeless. They were Cassius (Gaius Cassius Longinus), Brutus (Marcus Junius Brutus), and Decimus (Decimus Junius Brutus Albinus). Cassius, a general and senator, had several motives for wanting Caesar dead. In addition to fearing Caesar's ambition, he had been passed over for several leading positions and faced embarrassing rumors that Caesar had slept with his wife. When Cassius began to seek out co-conspirators, he found he could organize the conspiracy but lacked the boldness to lead it. For leadership, he needed a man of honor trusted by the people. Brutus, who came from one of the oldest families in the Republic, had the pedigree to do this. Prior to the establishment of the Roman Republic, Brutus's ancestor, also named Brutus (Lucius Junius Brutus), led the rebellion that overthrew the last king. As the numbers of conspirators grew, they began a public campaign to win over Brutus. This campaign included graffiti plastered everywhere, calling for a real Brutus to reveal himself. The public campaign, combined with powerful persuasion from Cassius, drove Brutus to turn against Caesar. It was rumored that Caesar believed Brutus might have been his son. During the time of Brutus's birth, Caesar, a notable ladies' man, was having an affair with Brutus's mother, Servilia. In Caesar's first consulship, he bought her a pearl that cost a small fortune and some other presents. He significantly reduced the price of some fine estates for her in a public auction. Because of his affection for Servilia, Caesar may have had a fondness for Brutus and may have forgiven him for supporting Pompey in the Civil War. Caesar would never suspect Brutus.

Decimus was the final puzzle piece. He was a close friend of Caesar's and, with Caesar's blessing, rose in the ranks to general. He was one of the few who had the dictator's full confidence. He should have been grateful to Caesar, but in a culture where the concepts of dignity, worth, prestige, and honor were the cherished ideal, a life spent in Caesar's shadow rendered Decimus's support wavering.

The three conspirators enlisted about 60 men to join them, including former military veterans who felt they were inadequately compensated for their service and those angered by Caesar's clemency for his enemies. They did not want to see their former enemies simply forgiven and raised to equals. For secrecy reasons, the conspirators met in small groups at private homes and avoided the usual conspiracy ritual of taking pledges over sacrificed animals.

They had barely a month to act, as Caesar was leaving for a military campaign on March 18 and would be surrounded by his vast army.

There were many discussions and proposals while they investigated how and where to execute Caesar. Some recommended that it be done when he made his favorite walk to the top of Capitoline Hill and passed through some of the most important religious sites of the Forum. Another idea was for it to be done at the elections when he had to cross a bridge to appoint the magistrates in the very crowded public area called the Campus Martius. They discussed drawing lots to decide who would push him from the bridge and who would run up and kill him. Another plan was to wait for a coming gladiatorial show. The advantage of the show was that no suspicion would be aroused if weapons were seen being prepared for the assassination. In the end, they decided to kill Caesar in the Senate House. They felt it would be the safest place since no arms were allowed in the Senate, and they wanted to kill Caesar publicly. Caesar also felt safe in the Senate House and would not suspect anything. He did not typically take his bodyguard into the Senate House. Caesar had fought in dozens of significant battles as a professional soldier and was absolutely not afraid of Senators sworn to protect him.

A meeting was scheduled for Caesar to attend the Senate on March 15. It was supposed to be a routine visit with nothing important to discuss, although a rumor spread that a proposal to crown Caesar king might be presented. That morning, Calpurnia, awoke from a nightmare in which she saw her husband murdered, maybe a result of her recalling a dire warning by a popular soothsayer named Spurinna, and she begged Caesar not to attend the meeting. He finally gave in to his wife's bad feelings and cancelled his meeting at the Senate after he ran into Spurinna again.

"The Ides of March have come, and I'm still here," said a smug Caesar.

The soothsayer responded, "Aye, the day has come, but it is not gone." It was a bad omen.

The undeterred conspirators had to persuade Caesar to change his mind. His close friend Decimus was chosen for the task. In a last act of betrayal, Decimus, who had served Caesar closely for more than a decade and was subsequently rewarded well for his efforts, visited Caesar at his home. He told the ruler that he should not risk showing any fear in the eyes of the Senate. He convinced Caesar that if he failed to show for the meeting, the Senators would look at him as either a tyrant or a weakling. He also mocked the soothsayer and the dream of Caesar's wife, saying, "Will someone of your position listen to the dreams of a woman and the omens of a foolish man?" Decimus's prodding worked, and Caesar headed toward the Senate House as a lamb led to slaughter.

Before Caesar entered the Senate House, the priests brought up the animal that would be sacrificed. The omens were clearly unfavorable by examining the internal organs of the animal. After this unsuccessful sacrifice, the priests made repeated attempts to see if anything more favorable might appear than what had already been revealed. In the end, they said they could not clearly see the divine intent, but there was a deadly spirit hidden in the sacrificial animals. Caesar was disturbed and abandoned foretelling until just before sunset, although the priests continued with their efforts. The conspirators who were present were delighted at the omens but not happy that Caesar's friends begged him to put off the meeting of the Senate because of what the priests had said.

Caesar agreed to postpone his visit to the Senate House, but Brutus persuaded him not to listen to the blathering of priests but to listen to what he felt. He built up Caesar's ego and then took him by the right hand and led him to the Senate, which was quite near. Caesar confidently followed in silence.

It was about noon when Caesar entered the Senate House. The Senators rose when they saw Caesar enter the room. Caesar took his seat on a golden chair facing the Senate. If Caesar was nervous about any bad omens, it did not show. His face was a pillar of confidence. Those who were to take part in the assassination stood in a row closest to Caesar with their hidden daggers tucked under their togas. Tillius Cimber, sweating with nervousness, approached Caesar in a hurry. He grabbed Caesar's toga and locked his hands on Caesar's wrists.

"My brother whom you exiled is remorseful. I implore you to allow him to come home to his family and serve you. I beg of you!"

Caesar tried to free himself and use his hands but was prevented by Cimber. He became extremely irritated. That was the moment the conspirators wanted to make their move. All the conspirators quickly unsheathed their daggers and rushed at Caesar. Publius Servilius Casca, a friend of Caesar's and an experienced killer, was given the glory of the first blow. Casca swung his knife toward Caesar's neck but stabbed him in the chest instead. Caesar, a competent veteran of many battles, now fought desperately to defend himself.

Caesar cried, "Why, this is violence!" Caesar caught Casca's arm, ran it through with his stylus, and managed to swat Casca away, but the blows from assailants were without mercy. Casca's brother, Gaius Casca, delivered the second blow, which struck the dictator in the ribs, and other attackers crowded in, encircling Caesar and stabbing his body. Caesar thrashed weakly as key conspirators got shots in, with Cassius planting a glancing blow across his face, Decimus striking deep under his ribs, and Brutus, who himself received an accidental slash across the hand from Cassius in the melee, connecting with Caesar's thigh. Every conspirator made sure to take part in the assassination, and each of them managed to stab Caesar. The mutilated body was a horrible and bloody scene.

Under the mass of wounds, Caesar crawled to the foot of Pompey's statue and breathed his last. After the assassination, Marcus Brutus immediately turned to the Senate and pleaded with them that everything was okay. He then explained his reasons for the death of the tyrant. Brutus's prepared speech fell on deaf ears. The frightened Senators did not understand what was happening and quickly fled the Senate House, likely fearing for their own safety. Soon, panic struck throughout Rome, and the conspirators raced off to Capitoline Hill where they could safely hole up against the anger of the Roman mob.

Caesar's body lay on the Senate floor, lifeless for some time, and finally, three common slaves put him on a litter and carried him home with one of his arms hanging off the litter. Originally, the conspirators intended to destroy Caesar's legacy, void all his decrees, and drag his corpse to the Tiber, but they feared Caesar's loyal defenders. Caesar's loyal supporter Marcus Aemilius Lepidus, known as Lepidus, was serving as Caesar's master of the horse and began taking control of the streets after the assassination. The master of the horse was an appointed position similar to a captain of arms. Lepidus would maintain order on the streets of Rome with force until the situation there settled down.

CHAPTER V
TENSION AND UNREST

Liborius had just finished his afternoon tasks and was waiting for one of the fullones, or laundry workers, to visit and take the household urine. The fullones collected the city's important urine supply and paid for it. The Romans had many uses for urine, including cleaning, whitening teeth, and laundry. Standing with the bucket outside the door, Lucius charged in, nearly spilling the valuable liquid. A red-faced Lucius, beside himself with anger, yelled to Liborius, "Fetch my sword and armor." Liborius did it immediately, calming himself with an effort. Lucius explained to Liborius that Caesar had been murdered and they were going without delay to Caesar's home to see what they could learn and provide help, if needed. Liborius assisted Lucius quickly, putting on his armor and setting out at once.

A certain tension was in the air between the factions of the conspirators and Caesar's loyal supporters. The legionnaires were the most upset. For many, all they owned was because of Caesar and his generosity. Along a quiet street in Rome, Lucius and Liborius walked by a tall and gaunt man singing to himself loudly, "Caesar led the Gauls in triumph, led them to the Senate House. Then the Gauls took off their pants and put on the laticlave." The laticlave was a purple band on the fore part of the tunic worn by senators; it was an emblem of office. This man was clearly in support of the conspirators. Anger roared in Lucius. His eyes narrowed to slits. He trembled with fury, his hands clenched tightly, and then charged, tackling the man. He then began to beat the man senseless. Liborius looked upon the man with sympathy, lowering his head. Lucius, blind with fury, pulled out his gladius and was poised to kill the man. The man cried out, begging for mercy. Lucius's eyes locked directly with the man's eyes and then softened. Lucius took in a deep breath and then released his gladius. He scabbarded it and then walked away, ignoring the man. Liborius caught up to his master, and they walked in silence.

As they approached Caesar's home, they saw a young woman on a dirt path that led to the villa. She was walking away from the entrance. Above her elbows were armlets fashioned like coiled asps and linked at the wrists by strands of gold. Her small head sat on her long, graceful neck. She placed her hands over her face and began sobbing. As they drew closer, they noticed it was Cleopatra, tears streaming down her face and her son, Caesarion, clutching her arms. "Your father has left you nothing," she whispered to the boy. Liborius and Lucius looked away from her, paying no attention to the woman who had caused so much scandal in Rome, and proceeded to the heavily guarded entry. One of the guards at the door, a former veteran of the Tenth Legion, quickly noticed Lucius and allowed him to enter with Liborius.

The villa was crowded with many of Caesar's supporters whose worried faces filled the air with great anxiety over the magnitude of Caesar's death. Lucius swiftly probed for as much information as he could gather from the angry veterans. Caesar's body was transported by slaves to his humble villa, and the family gathered there to mourn and discuss what would happen next. Caesar's will was fetched by Caesar's father-in-law, Lucius Calpurnius Piso, from the Vestal Virgins who stored all the wills in Rome. He had just returned and just finished reading it out loud to the family. In great shock, they heard that Caesar's heir would be his sister's 18-year-old grandson Octavius, a virtually unknown great-nephew. Legally, Octavius would be adopted as Caesar's son and would now be called Julius Caesar Octavianus, or Octavian. Octavian would inherit three-fourths of his uncle's estate. Further appalling was that the remaining wealth would go to the Roman people. The family, including Cleopatra, would get nothing significant. Cleopatra and her entourage would return to Egypt with nothing for Caesarion.

"Make way for Pontifex Maximus and the Consul of Rome!" a guard shouted. A small commotion resulted as Mark Antony, loyal follower of Caesar and now chief priest of Rome, walked into the crowded villa. In a simple act of self-preservation, he had fled after the assassination to Pompey's theater adjacent to the Senate House, discarding his consular robe to try to maintain anonymity for personal protection. When Lepidus finally brought the streets under control, Mark Antony made his way to Caesar's home. His friends quickly brought him up-to-date, and he sat reading the will. With a grimace, he read about his small inheritance and that he would not be Caesar's chosen heir. The grimace quickly turned to a calm look, and he rose and addressed the crowded villa: "We must be calm during this time of turmoil. Mob rule shall not rule Caesar's beloved Rome. Please return to your homes. It is what Caesar would have wanted." The crowd was moved by the heartfelt speech, and Caesar's supporters, as well as Liborius and Lucius, slowly departed the villa to return home.

The return trip to Rome was uneventful for Liborius and Lucius. They patiently waited for news as events unfolded after Caesar's death. One morning, Liborius awoke to a hand shaking his shoulder, and he looked up and saw Lucius. "Awake! We have work to do," Lucius spoke with a hint of mischief. As Liborius got out of bed, Lucius handed him a gladius and said, "As funny as the incident was with that would-be mugger, I feel it would be useful for you to learn to protect yourself." Lucius then pulled out a straw dummy he had created to represent an enemy combatant. He taught Liborius some basic drills, stabbing the dummy in specific vital areas and instructing Liborius to practice the same drills. The gladius wasn't a flashy weapon. It was simple but designed to kill quickly and efficiently by stabbing. Its primary function was to gut the enemy and move on to the next. Liborius was clumsy with the weapon at first, but it did not take him long to learn the drills. By the time Lucius was confident that Liborius understood the drills, Liborius was drenched in sweat, soaking his tunic. His muscles burned from motions he had never made before. Liborius was grateful for the morning training and thanked Lucius. Although it was not forbidden, teaching a slave how to fight, particularly with a sword, did not happen very often. Liborius was passionate about his training and would become a great student.

As the nights went by, the people could feel the atmosphere of Rome about to burst. Caesar had ended a brutal civil war with victory, and now his death would most likely spark a new one. Lucius's desire to settle down seemed only a dream now as he prepared mentally to put on his uniform again in service to his empire.

CHAPTER VI
CAESAR'S PYRE

A crack of thunder crashed in the hollowing wind, followed by a downpour of rain over Rome. Lucius stood motionless as water dripped over his face from his soaked hair. He was consumed with the memory of Caesar. The rainwater helped him mourn, as if the water would wash away the tears of his heart. Time stood still, and he was soaked to the bone. Caesar was gone, but his memory was strong. The Roman Empire had lost leaders before, but this time, the people were shaken to the core. There had never before been a leader like Caesar. He was loved by the common people, and that love had now been disturbed. There would be hell to pay, for nothing is more powerful than love.

On March 16, the Senate wisely gathered to settle the affairs of Rome and prevent an uprising. In this conference, Lepidus argued fiercely against the conspirators who sought to destroy Caesar's legacy. Cicero, however, known as one of the greatest Roman orators, convinced the Senate to compromise in order to save the Republic from civil war. The assassins, or so-called liberators, were given amnesty. To receive that amnesty, they were forced to uphold all Caesar's laws and individual honors, and the terms included the concession that Caesar's soldiers would receive everything they had been promised.

The Senate, fearing that violence would spread, gave the major conspirators provincial governorships. That would not only protect them from the Roman mob by sending them away from the city but would also grant them hefty influence and the right to control Roman legions. Cassius, the leading force behind the plot, was given Africa. Decimus, the man who finally convinced Caesar to make the final walk to the site of his death, was given Cisalpine Gaul at the southern border with Gaul. That area had been a favorite of Caesar's for recruiting legionnaires, and he had rewarded them with full Roman citizenship. Brutus, the infamous betrayer, was appointed to Crete, a small eastern province.

You may have thought Antony was the biggest loser since he received a meager inheritance and his enemies were now in power. But Antony, in a brilliant stroke of political genius that would have made his mentor Caesar proud, completely turned the tables on the conspirators. He secured the right to deliver the eulogy at Caesar's funeral. Though Cassius vehemently opposed the idea of a grand public funeral, Brutus argued that the average Roman citizen needed closure, thereby allowing Antony to have his way. What Brutus didn't realize was that Antony, over the course of the grand and highly emotional funeral, would take the opportunity to turn Rome upside down.

Liborius and Lucius were in the crowd to listen to Antony's speech. They had found a small location filled with loyal veterans of the Tenth Legion. The crowds were enormous, but with a gladius displayed at their sides, Lucius and Liborius were able to secure an area. From their position, they were able to catch a glimpse of Antony and were able to hear him speak. The veterans, angry at Caesar's death, still longed for vengeance. They told stories of Caesar that they remembered from their many military campaigns. Many of the stories Liborius had never heard. Caesar, unlike most generals, suffered alongside his men on the march as well as in combat. He would often lead from the front, sometimes on horseback but most often on foot, with his bare head exposed in all kinds of weather. When the issue was doubtful, he sent away the horses, his own among the first, to impose upon the troops the need to stand their ground by taking away the aid to flight. He would then put on his purple robe, which no one could miss in the thick of the fighting, turning certain defeat into victory. He would stop those who fled, keep others in their ranks, and seize men by the throat, turning them again toward the enemy.

The mournful veterans turned to the pyre erected in the center of Rome near the tomb of Julia, the beloved daughter of Caesar. The men looked upon the dias at a gilded shrine, a model of the Temple of Venus, giving credit to the goddess from whom Caesar claimed divinity. Inside, all could see the blood-soaked robe that Caesar had been slain in. The funeral began, and a herald took the platform, reciting the decree of the Senate in which it gave honors to Caesar. Then he read the oaths of all those who had pledged his personal safety. The list was long. Caesar was being anointed by the government as a god. Liborius did not understand much about the gods or religion but questioned in his heart how a man, although an incredible general, could gain divinity.

A trumpet was blown brief and shrill. Antony walked up to the pyre and turned to the crowd. He coughed and then proclaimed, "My fellow Romans! Words cannot give credit to our beloved Caesar who has been taken so unjustly from us. No one will ever dispute how much he loved you and how much he loved Rome." Antony then went on to sing the praises of Caesar. Next, in a choked voice, Antony read the will of Caesar. Caesar left money to every citizen of Rome, and the vast, private garden near the Tiber River would be turned into a public park for everyone to enjoy. With the crowd glued to his words, Antony prepared to make a powerful, political statement.

Antony then began to attack Caesar's assassins with a brilliantly crafted speech. He cried out aloud, "Of what account, O Caesar, was your humanity, of what account your honor, of what account the laws? Nay, although you created many laws to protect the person, you yourself have been cut down by your so-called friends. Now a victim of murder, you lie dead at the Forum while the assassins are free to destroy what you have given to the Roman people. Woe to those who have soaked your robes with blood. The people will never forget Caesar's love for them."

Upon finishing the speech, with tears in his eyes, Antony held up the robe Caesar had worn when he was murdered. When the crowd saw the stab-shredded, bloody garment, they were instantly overcome with a need for vengeance. As Caesar's funeral pyre burned, the mob took up torches from it and went off to burn down the estates of the conspirators who were involved in the assassination. Liborius and Lucius joined the mob with Caesar's veterans. They watched as the destructive fires roared through the dry, wooden structures of the conspirators' estates. Fortunately, the fires were contained and did not spread into the city. The mob had their revenge. Before long, the so-called liberators were forced to flee the city, faced with certain death at the hands of the mob. Antony was given a well-fought victory and now was recognized as the people's champion.

As for the great Caesar, his bones were carried away and laid to rest in the family tomb, and a shrine was later erected at the funeral pyre. A great fire was lit for sacrifice, and the veterans of the legions threw in the war souvenirs with which they had adorned themselves for the funeral. Many of the women offered up the jewels they had worn and their children's amulets and robes. To the people of Rome, Caesar was a great hero. In July 44 BC, a great comet appeared in the sky at Caesar's funeral games as if to show Caesar's soul departing this world. To the people of the ancient world, this was a great sign of Caesar's ascendancy into heaven to take his place among the gods. Caesar brought wealth and power to Rome, and the people loved him for it. To them, Caesar truly was a god. In January 42 BC, Gaius Julius Caesar was named Divus (Divine) Julius by the Senate, officially confirming him as a god of the Roman people.

Lucius returned home with his faithful slave, Liborius, and waited patiently to be called back to military service. Liborius polished and cleaned Lucius's armor. The mostly iron armor was heavy and needed to be strong and in good shape. This time, Lucius personally sharpened his gladius on a whetstone. He worked for hours until the blade was razor sharp. As he sharpened, he reflected on his life. Lucius had come a long way from being a simple farmer in the Roman province of Baetica. He had sold the farm before he entered his service and wondered what it looked like today. He had achieved wealth in his service to Rome and would forever have the respect of its citizens. His body was remarkably healthy and fit after his many years of campaigning.

A Roman soldier might be envisioned as a brave man, standing and waiting for the onslaught of mighty foes, but the Roman soldier was, above all, a man. And, like most men, he felt a need for a woman's companionship. Most civilians in the empire married between the ages of 15 and 20, and if Lucius naturally had his eye on a particular girl, she would not have waited for him. His military service by law prevented him from marriage until he retired. It was considered ideal for a Roman soldier to not have a romantic relationship in times of war, for it was thought it would make him more aggressive and energetic in combat. The seldom-enforced law did not prevent Roman soldiers from having relationships, and almost all soldiers had a woman of one sort or another in their lives, either a common-law wife or the use of female slaves and prisoners who followed the army in baggage trains. Lucius would retire one day to marry and have many children, a belief he held strongly in his heart for countless years.

After the mob riots, an uneasy calm settled on Rome, and Lepidus continued to control the streets of Rome. Patrols of armed men, mostly former legionnaires, maintained order. The most important area, the Forum, the center of local government and the main marketplace for the city, was guarded well. In the Forum was a table where standard weights and measures could be verified. It was designed to protect people from being cheated when doing business. Commerce continued smoothly in Rome. Farmers were still able to bring their produce to the city to trade for other goods or coins. The wealthy Romans who typically worked a six-hour day in the city from sunrise to noon were still able to spend their afternoons at leisure, enjoying the city baths or the games.

To amuse himself and help cope with the anguish of Caesar's death, Lucius decided to see a gladiatorial game at a wooden amphitheater hastily built just outside Rome. He thought the entertainment by gladiators, loved by the masses, would provide an excellent escape. The professional fighters would risk their lives and limbs for the crowd, enduring smashed teeth, broken noses, and all manner of injury. Liborius was excited that Lucius would bring him along. With Lucius's military rank and coin, they were able to get good seats with a fine view of the arena.

The morning events, which included animals trained to perform tricks, were followed by a lunch break when patrons could leave the arena to satisfy their hunger. Liborius and Lucius did not linger and went off to find some fresh bread and fish from the vendors outside the arena. Those who lingered were entertained with the execution of common criminals. In cruel irony, the deaths were made to match the method of the crimes they had committed. Murderers were thrown unprotected to wild beasts, and those who had committed arson were burned alive.

Liborius and Lucius returned for the afternoon entertainment, devoted to the main event, the gladiators' combat. Liborius was aware that the majority were slaves, enslaved like himself during the numerous wars Rome fought to expand its territory. He knew they were treated relatively well and received extensive training. It would be interesting to see the gladiators who trained with exotic weapons such as the three-pronged spear known as the trident. Although Liborius thought he admired the gladiators, he was grateful that he would not be participating in the arena. The event was plain butchery, no rules beyond no eye-gouging or biting. "Kill him! Flog him!" the bloodthirsty spectators roared. "Why does he fall so easily?" "Why is he such a mouse?" Liborius watched the blood and gore and wondered how men could be that cruel. Queasiness rose in his stomach as the gruesome display continued. Blood drained from his face, and he sweated in an attempt not to throw up.

Liborius abhorred the senseless deaths. He reasoned that combat in war was different. In war, you defended your people or served them, but combat for entertainment purposes was wrong. Not all fights were to the death. When a gladiator was about to lose, he could cry out for mercy. Liborius learned that thumbs down signified swords down, which meant the losing gladiator was worth more to them alive and was to be spared to fight another day. Lucius could see Liborius struggling and decided they would leave before the last few matches. Both men returned home. They would never return to the gladiatorial games.

Lucius continued to go out for drinks and food and converse with his veteran brothers-in-arms. It was his favorite evening routine. As a well-known centurion, he was also invited to formal dinner parties, reclining on couches around a low table. The wealthy Romans entertained their dinner guests with dancers, poets, and musicians. Lucius enjoyed all that Rome had to offer. He envisioned Rome as a great place to start a family one day. Liborius lingered behind, keeping the small flat in good order and doing his menial work without complaint. Leaving home only to fetch food and household necessities was never stimulating or thrilling. Liborius was eager to go back on campaign with Lucius again and hoped the call for the legions would be heard soon.

Liborius continued to practice with his gladius and took pride in his new skill. It was also an escape from his rather boring life. He had many restless nights contemplating his circumstances and continued desire to join the military as a legionnaire serving Rome. One thought continued to bother him. He respected Caesar and knew Caesar as a great man but could not comprehend why he was confirmed a god. Did not an auriga, a slave with gladiator status, whisper, "You are only a man" in Caesar's ear during the triumph so Caesar would not lose his sense of perspective? Liborius thought Caesar was truly special and had some favor with the gods, but he doubted that Caesar should be one of them.

Romans lived in a world where there was a god for almost anything, and they attempted to communicate with them all the time. Romans had a history of manipulating religious doctrine for political purposes and did not always take it seriously. They had many gods and little actual faith. Lucius was not overly religious, but, like most Romans, he considered ritual observances of omens important. To Lucius, Caesar was completely cocky and confident in himself and ignored the omens and signs of his death. Because of Caesar's ignorance, his destiny was sealed. If Caesar had somehow understood the warnings correctly or listened to his wife, his fate would be completely different. A god, Caesar was not.

CHAPTER VII
AVENGE CAESAR

T he early morning sun rose over the beaches of Appollonia just outside northwestern Greece. The smell of the sea was carried on the cool ocean breeze. Octavian stood barefoot in the wet sand, dressed in a simple woolen tunic. He had just received news that interrupted his military training. The 17-year old teenager was informed that his great-uncle on his mother's side was dead and that the will posthumously made him the adopted son of Caesar. This was a surprise, although Octavian was Caesar's closest male heir. Octavian barely knew Caesar, but he knew of his fame and legacy. He needed to get to Rome quickly to secure his inheritance and take his place as Caesar's chosen successor.

Octavian finally arrived in Rome. Liberators or conspirators, whatever you prefer to call them, were forced to flee the city, faced with certain death. Octavian was advised not to accept Caesar's bequest because he was so young and ill prepared to deal with the hazards of Roman politics. Nevertheless, he did accept it. Caesar's will called for games for public entertainment. They required funds, but Mark Antony supervised Caesar's funds and refused to grant

Octavian access to them. Octavian borrowed funds to comply with Caesar's will, and his efforts garnered public support for him. His efforts to fulfill Caesar's will began to gain him considerable support among Caesar's veterans and common Roman citizens.

Mark Antony was defying the will of the Senate, and they, led by Cicero, called upon Octavian for support against Antony. The Senate made Octavian a senator even though he was far too young to qualify. Octavian's troops joined with the legions the Senate had at its command. The combined forces easily drove Antony out of Italy into Gaul. In the battle with Antony's forces, the two elected consuls of Rome were killed. The Senate, in order to gain favor with Octavian, conferred the title of consul on him and officially recognized Octavian as the son and heir of Julius Caesar.

Great political and social turmoil continued in Rome, threatening to destroy it. Octavian, in an unexpected decision, chose to align himself with Lepidus and Antony. In 43 BC, they established the Second Triumvirate with dictatorial powers that would last for five years. The three of them immediately set to work to crush any remaining opposition in the Senate. They agreed to eliminate those senators and members of the Roman aristocracy that any one of the three considered a threat to public order. Hundreds of senators were executed and their properties confiscated due to their supposed support, mostly for the conspirators' forces. Under this arrangement, Antony designated Cicero for execution even though he had supported Octavian, argued against tryranny, and supported the restoration of the Republic. It was rumored that Fulvia, Antony's wife, vented her hatred for the dead orator as well. Supposedly, she took Cicero's lifeless head in her hands and spat on it. Then, setting it on her knees, she opened the mouth and with pins from her hair pierced the tongue that had argued so vehemently against her husband. The Second Triumvirate was without a doubt all-powerful and, most importantly, had the support of the army.

Two of the principal conspirators, Brutus and Cassius, had fled and taken control of the eastern provinces. There, they raised a large army consisting of the eastern legions and relying on taxes from local kingdoms allied to Rome. To counter this, the members of the Second Triumvirate in Rome—Octavian, Antony, and Lepidus—raised their own army to defeat the conspirators and avenge Caesar's death. Caesar's retired legions were itching to fight. Legions were quickly assembled, and Lepidus resurrected the Tenth Legion. The Tenth and 27 other legions were ready to march and utterly destroy the conspirators.

Lucius, a loyal soldier of Rome, did not hesitate and answered the call to reassemble. He took a grateful Liborius immediately to the assembly camp of the Tenth Legion just outside Rome. It would take time for the veterans to report, but they did, indeed. There were a few hundred at first, and then thousands made the journey. Liborius quickly returned to his former camp routine of maintaining his master's equipment and preparing meals. Supplies were plentiful so close to Rome, and the legion did not go lacking. As the summer ended, the legion was at full strength with a few volunteers taken from around Rome to fill the ranks. The entire Roman Army was to ferry across the Adriatic first, sending out a scouting force of eight legions commanded by two veteran commanders, Gaius Norbanus Flaccus and Lucius Decidius Saxa. After the advance, Antony and Octavian would each take forces of the remaining legions and follow them. Lepidus was to remain behind in Italy to hold the home front. The Tenth Legion, Caesar's favorite, was chosen to lead the advanced scouting force.

The Tenth Legion was to be ferried on merchant ships that used mainly wind power. The merchant ships were built to transport heavy cargo with double planking that strengthened their hulls. They operated with giant sails and a small triangular sail called the supparum at the bow. Departure morning was a cloudy, overcast day that grew darker as rain clouds moved in. Thunder roared in the distance, and it began to rain heavily. The rain pounded them and drenched the men from head to toe. The Tenth had hoped for better weather to depart but had no such luck. The order was given to load the ships. Just before departure, the army prayed and sacrificed a bull to Neptune, the god of the sea, for safe passage ashore.

It seems their prayers were not answered. The journey was miserable for the legionnaires as they crossed the long stretch of water. The soldiers were packed in the cargo holds with just enough room to lie down. Liborius and Lucius sat together, enduring the misery. Liborius had never been on a ship before, and Lucius had traveled by ship only a few times. With the ship rocking back and forth on the waves, Liborius's face turned pale, and he felt light-headed and dizzy. He broke out in a cold sweat and could not hold back his stomach as he became nauseated. Before he knew it, he vomited in pain, causing a chain reaction by many captive voyagers. He continued to retch uncontrollably, and the feeling of weakness and nausea continued until the ship arrived at its destination. In what hinted like forever, the ships began to arrive off the coast of Greece.

The Tenth Legion quickly departed from the ships and began to unload their equipment. Liborius worked tirelessly bringing supplies on shore as the day turned to evening. After one ship was unloaded, he went to the next one without stopping. The rain had finally ceased, but the wind was brutal and made him shiver. It was dark when the last of the supplies was unloaded. By firelight, the weary travelers set up a quick camp so they could rest. Liborius went to receive their ration of wine and water it down. Reducing the wine to one-third, he added a bit of vinegar and additional water with a little honey available to make posca, the main drink of the Roman Army. It was a very appreciated drink and kept the legionnaires walking in extreme conditions. They would never drink the wine full strength because being drunk on duty was a death sentence. For food, Liborius pulled out some salted mutton. After serving his master, Liborius quickly consumed his meal and then set up his master's cart for sleeping. Lucius wasted no time dropping himself on the cart and quickly dozing off. Liborius finished unpacking what he needed for morning preparations and then, exhausted, went to sleep.

Norbanus and Saxa, the leaders of the advance, did not waste any time and immediately set off on their mission. Passing the town of Philippi in eastern Macedonia, a province of Greece, they found the conspirator forces taking a strong defensive position at a narrow mountain pass. It appeared that Brutus and Cassius wanted to avoid a general engagement, preferring to operate on the defensive. The conspirators fortified their position with ditches and ramparts straddling an important Roman road called the Via Egnatia and placed Brutus's troops to the north of the road and Cassius's troops to the south. The Triumvirate scouting force, including the Tenth Legion, waited as Antony's troops joined them, with Antony arranging his men opposite Cassius. Octavian arrived in Greece but was delayed at Dyrrachium because of his ill health, but he managed to join the army regardless and faced his forces opposite Brutus.

Eager to begin fighting, Antony tried several times to bring about a traditional Roman battle, but Cassius and Brutus would not advance from behind their defenses. Seeking to break the standoff, Antony began looking for a way through the marshes in an effort to surprise Cassius. Finding no path through the marsh, he began constructing a causeway. Quickly guessing the enemy's intentions, Cassius began building fortifications to stop the causeway and turned his forces south in an effort to cut off Antony's men in the marshes. This struggle became the First Battle of Philippi on October 3, 42 BC. Antony's men made it through the marsh and quickly overran the fortifications. Driving through Cassius's men, Antony's troops demolished the ramparts and ditch and put the enemy to rout. Seizing the camp, Antony's men then repelled other units from Cassius's command as they moved north from the marshes.

Watching the battle unfold in the south, Brutus attacked Octavian's army from the north. Fortune was with his commander, Marcus Cornvinus, who assaulted the camp and captured three legionary standards. Octavian was forced to retreat into a mucky swamp as Brutus's men plundered the tents for spoils. This time, fortune switched to Octavian because Brutus's men did not follow up their attack. Octavian's forces would live to fight another day. Cassius, the best military mind for Brutus, did not see victory for Brutus and moved his forces back.

Brutus delayed further battle over the next few weeks while Antony pushed through the marshes, forcing Brutus to stretch his position. This delay caused Brutus's allies to become irate and forced Brutus to engage the enemy in bloodshed. Surging forth on October 23, Brutus's men met Octavian and Antony in battle. Fighting in close quarters, the battle proved very grisly, and the Triumvirate forces succeeded in repelling Brutus's attack. As his men began retreating, Octavian and his army pushed forward and captured their camp. Brutus's army was completely routed. In shame, Brutus chose to go the honorable way and committed suicide.

CHAPTER VIII

ROAD TO RECOVERY

I t was morning, and the fog hung low over the battlefield, clinging to the earth. Liborius was at camp stacking wood when Urban, a legionnaire under Lucius's command, told him the grim news that Lucius had been led back to camp, heavily wounded from the fighting. The medicus vulnerarius, known as wound doctors, picked him up in the field with other wounded during the battle and sent him via ambulance into one of the two receiving battlefield hospital tents located on opposite sides of the field that moved with the army. Octavian had recently attached the medicus vulnerarius medical unit to the army. Once Lucius was in the hospital tent, the surgeon started working on him. He was in great hands, for the military surgeons were only second to the prized surgeons who repaired valuable gladiators. They were also competent on how to press, pull, and tug their patients' bodies and limbs back into good alignment. Lucius had broken his arm and had severe deep cuts from the fighting. The broken arm was set, and stitches were used to sew up the cuts. The tent had a range of surgical tools that were usually boiled in vessels before an operation started. Although they didn't understand why, it helped prevent infection.

Lucius was favored and received expert care due to his military service. Most people, especially the poor, did not have such care since diseases were regarded as an affliction of the gods that required prayer, sacrifice, and pagan rites to alleviate. Many entered temples and spent the night in prayer to the gods, hoping to receive a cure. Doctors made rounds doing what little they could. Fortunately, Lucius would recover and would not have to visit the house of the dying or infirm that many wounded veterans were pensioned to. It was several days before Lucius was brought to his personal tent to mend. He lay in his cart in serious discomfort. Liborius administered willow tea that the medicus vulnerarius provided for Lucius to drink. This foul-tasting brew was to help reduce fever and alleviate pain. Liborius took great care of his master, attending to his prolonged recovery.

It would be several weeks before Lucius was ready to take back his command as a centurion. Lucius was to stay behind with the other wounded in Greece until he could rejoin the army. The main army and the Tenth were sailing back to Italy. With the death of Cassius and Brutus at the Battle of Philippi, the Second Triumvirate essentially ended major resistance to their rule and succeeded in avenging the death of Julius Caesar. Octavian, Lepidus, and Antony strengthened their bond with the Pact of Brundisium, which split the territory among them. Italy was to be shared among the Triumvirate. Lepidus's possession of the provinces of Hispania and lower Gaul was confirmed, and he agreed to hand over seven legions to Antony and Octavian. Antony retained control of most of Gaul, and Octavian held Africa. Octavian's share of territory was practically humiliating. All the most important provinces went to Antony and Lepidus, although the deal to transfer Lepidus's legions meant that Lepidus could be effectively eliminating himself as an equal partner in the future.

However, the fighting was not over; they had to manage the menace of Sextus Pompey, son of Pompey. Sextus controlled the provinces of Sicily, Corsica, and Sardinia, which provided much of Rome's grain supply. Sextus's navy regularly intercepted Roman shipping, leading to problems with the grain supply, which could ultimately bring Rome to famine. Lepidus raised a large army of 14 legions and a considerable navy to counter Sextus and was eager to attack. Antony would remain in the East, while Octavian's returning forces from Greece would join Lepidus and put an end to Sextus and the last of the resistance.

After the army of Octavian departed from Greece, what was left of the military camp was very quiet except for an occasional scream from the hospital tent as the medicus vulnerarius worked. Lucius continued to heal and eventually could stand on his feet with the assistance of Liborius who was ready to catch him if he fell. In a few weeks, Lucius was able to go for short walks. He pushed himself hard physically to aid in his quick recovery, sometimes falling over from exertion. Most nights he turned in early, sleeping soundly in his cart from exhaustion. Liborius had plenty of free time in the evenings and enjoyed sitting around the campfire hearing stories from the men recovering from their wounds. After the fires died out, he lay down and watched the twinkling stars. He heard two points of view about the night sky. There was a sphere or bowl over the earth, and the stars were light from heaven shining through holes in it, or the stars were gods themselves. Having been taken at a young age from his tribe, he did not know or understand well the gods of his ancestors. He was familiar with the Roman gods from his time with the Legion. He knew that Jupiter was king of the gods and that the Legion often prayed to Mars, the god of war, to grant them favor before battle. He would often ponder the gods. There seemed to be a god of everything, from the god of love to the god of wealth.

What interested him most about the gods was what he learned about life after death. Pluto was known as the god of the dead. Romans would not even speak Pluto's real name because they feared simply saying the name would get them a one-way ticket to the afterworld. Liborius had learned that when someone died, they traveled down to the underworld. First, they had to cross the River of the Dead, called the Styx, led by spirits. They had to pay the ferryman, Charon, with the coin they were buried with. Next, they had to get past Cerberus, a fierce dog with three heads that only let the dead through. They would then go before the three judges, Minos, Rhadamanthos, and Aeacus, who would ask them to account for their lives. After they made their accounting, they would be given the water of the River Lethe, the river of forgetfulness, to make them forget their past lives. Then they would be sent to the Elysian Fields, a version of paradise if they had been a warrior or hero. They would go to the plain of Asphodel if they had been good citizens and lived a good life. If they had offended the gods, they would go to Tartarus where they would be punished by the Furies in proportion to their crime. The Romans believed their empire rested on the Pax Deorum, which meant that if the Romans did right by the pagan gods, those deities would do right by them.

Every day, Lucius grew stronger until he was robust enough to fight. He exercised by practicing his shield and gladius drills with Liborius. While Lucius was recovering his strength, Liborius held back until they were able to train full force. Lucius found a group of recovering soldiers and staged mock fights, with one party trying to dislodge another party defended with shields. To completely recover, he needed to be able to march in full gear carrying a full pack. He wasted no time starting with short trips and then grinded his way to several miles. Lucius walked with a slight limp, but other than that, he felt ready to return to the army. A ship was sailing to collect the men who had recovered enough to fight so they could be linked back to the army, and Lucius did not doubt he would be on it. Lucius's progress was rewarded when he was determined fit by the medicus vulnerarius to rejoin the Legion. He would sail along with recovered veterans to Portus Iulius in Italy.

Finally, it was time to leave. On the night before the trip to Italy, Lucius joined Liborius at the campfire and sat by his side.

Both men were excited to leave the next day. As the dry, withered branches slowly burned, they listened to whispering hisses and sizzling pops and smelled the thick smoke of the flaming wood. The heat warmed them, and the orange flames celebrated with their wild, flickering dance. Lucius rubbed the top of his head briskly, wondering what to say.

He turned to Liborius. "My life almost ended . . . was it for the glory of the Empire? To avenge Caesar? For a better afterlife in the Elysian Fields? Life is short on this earth. I would like to think life has some meaning to this world. I have prayed to the gods for this meaning, but they never seem to listen." He sighed deeply. "It's been so many years since I left my homeland to join the Legion. I will not return to my homeland, so I have no family outside the army. I have wealth from campaigning but no family to share it with." His voice softened. "In a way, you have been like family to me, and I have watched you grow from a young boy to a young man. You have been a good and faithful servant. I'm thankful for your service, and I'm going to begin paying you a wage. When peace is restored, I plan to retire, marry, and start a family in Rome."

Liborius did not know how his life would change, but he locked eyes with Lucius and spoke with a smile. "Thank you for your generosity to pay me. You have always treated me fairly. I do not know any soldier more deserving of a wonderful retirement than you. I have no doubt you will find a great wife and enjoy a good life."

Lucius returned the smile and poked the fire with a long stick. Cool air blew in, and the heat from the campfire stole it before it ever reaching their bodies. As the night grew longer, they stopped adding to the fire and watched the wood slowly turn to red ashes. When the coals no longer glowed, Lucius left for bed. Liborius lingered a while longer and then succumbed to the call of sleep.

CHAPTER IX
ROWING FOR FREEDOM

The campaign against Sextus was not going well. Octavian nominally oversaw the campaign against Sextus, but the campaign was actually commanded by Octavian's good friend and leading general, Marcus Vipsanius Agrippa, who had recently helped secure the Triumvirate renewal for a second five-year term. Antony and Octavian had begun fighting, but Agrippa and intermediaries convinced them to agree once more to peace. Agrippa was serving as governor of southern Gaul when he was summoned back to Rome by Octavian to assume the consulship for 37 BC. Since Sextus had command of the sea on the coast of Italy, Agrippa's first care was to provide a safe harbor for Octavian's ships. He accomplished that by cutting through the strips of land in southern Italy and digging a channel to connect Lake Lucrinus to the sea in order to change it into a harbor named Portus Julius. The new harbor was used to train the infantry and build ships for upcoming naval battles against Sextus. The new ships were built much larger in order to carry many more infantry units that were being trained at the same time.

When the navy was ready, they attempted to take Sicily by force. But due to bad weather, they were defeated twice in naval battles off Messina, a harbor city in northeast Sicily separated from mainland Italy by the Strait of Messina. Octavian was sure his combined army with Lepidus had the manpower to destroy Sextus, but they needed more ships. He then arranged a meeting with Antony, who was planning to attack Parthia and needed troops. Parthia was governed by the Seleucid kings who were originally a Macedonian dynasty that ruled parts of the former Persian Empire. Antony agreed to deliver ships for the attack on Sextus in exchange for troops to fight the Parthians. In the bargain, Antony lent Octavian 120 ships under the command of Titus Statilius Taurus, for which Octavian was to give him 20,000 infantry recruited from northern Italy. The ships arrived, but there was a shortage of rowers. While Antony kept his part of the bargain, Octavian did not complete the exchange.

The sun sank lower in the sky as the ship carrying the recovered veterans arrived in Portus Julius. Lucius, along with the veterans, were welcomed with great excitement on the docks. The Tenth's fellow legionnaires were glad to have him back. Some in the Legion doubted Lucius would be able to recover from his wounds. Lucius and Liborius were quickly directed to the crowded barracks in Portus Julius that the Tenth occupied. The wooden barracks consisted of long blocks. A full century would occupy a single block, with the centurion commander living in his more elaborate accommodation at the end. The long shadows of the evening dissolved into the gathering darkness of nighttime as Lucius and Liborius were shown to the centurion suite they would occupy. Liborius found and lit a tallow candle made from rendered animal fat and placed it on a small table in the room. The candle burned with a steady yellow flame as they unpacked their equipment.

A gentle knock alerted them to a legionnaire named Marcus Verus who was familiar to Liborius. He brought a small dinner for

Lucius that he shared with Liborius. It was a kind of cake made of boiled eggs mixed with bread. Marcus stayed and filled Lucius in on what had happened during Lucius's absence from the Legion. What distressed Lucius was the feuding between Antony and Octavian. Lucius wiped crumbs from his mouth.

"The last thing we need is another civil war," Lucius spoke, shaking his head. "If you ask me, there's plenty of spoils for both of them." Marcus nodded his head in agreement. "You may thinking about when is the next battle for the tenth," Lucius added. "Soon enough we will fight with Agrippa and defeat Sextus."

"Maybe after victory, Antony and Octavian will come to even better terms," Marcus added dryly. Lucius, worn out from the trip to Portus Julius, dismissed Marcus and retired to bed. In command again, he would need his strength.

The next morning, Lucius took charge of his century. It did not take long for the grizzled veteran to be back to his old self. Every morning after breakfast, or Prandium, he gave his legionnaires their duties individually or in small groups. Lucius's orders might be to dig out a ditch, work in the stables, man the gateway, patrol the local villages, bring a wagonload of supplies from a nearby depot, and so on. Liborius would complete his normal daily tasks, which were relatively easy, and then assist the legionnaires. The only task he did not participate in was the drill on the ships where the Tenth trained in naval combat. They hooked a long plank with a spike onto practice enemy ships, using it as a bridge to board the enemy ship and transforming sea combat into a version of land combat where the Roman legionnaires had the upper hand.

Liborius headed to Lucius's suite one afternoon after Lucius told him that today's orders were for the legionnaires to pass flyers around town. A tall stack of flyers awaited him to bring to the optio, the second in command under Lucius, who would distribute them to the men. Liborius could read very little, but with the pictures, he was able to determine that rowers were needed for the ships and that any slaves who served would be given their freedom. Liborius, eyes wide, began to grin. He knew the truth that Roman warships were not rowed by slaves. Many ignorant people thought that in a galley, which is propelled primarily by rowing, you would hear the clank of slaves' chains and the crack of the overseer's whip. This was rarely true for the Romans. Like the Greeks, they had an ideology called civic militarism. It was believed that if you were a citizen, you had an obligation to fight for your state, and as a reward, you were entitled to political rights. Rowers on military Roman ships were mostly free men of the provinces, not slaves. Liborius tingled from his head to his toes and was about to pick up the large stack of flyers when he was startled.

"Liborius,'" Lucius spoke in a warm tone. "Here is your first pay that I promised." He placed a sestertius in Liborius's palm. This coin was equal to one-quarter of a denarius. "After you distribute the flyers to the men, I need you to visit the bakery and pick up some bread for me. I'm sick of eating these lousy biscuits."

As of late, the legionnaires were given plenty of tasteless *panis militaris castrensis* in their rations. Lucius handed him additional money for the bread and, with a smile, told Liborius to not return unless the important mission was accomplished. Liborius wanted to run, to shout, to tell Lucius about the flyer, but he held his emotions in check. It was not the time. Liborius picked up the large stack of flyers and moved as quickly as he could to find the optio under Lucius and hand him the flyers. He found the optio rolling dice in a board game with some men. Board games were popular entertainment for soldiers who spent hours playing them in order to kill time. He waited until the optio's turn was completed and then delivered the flyers to him. After delivering them, he exited the barracks and headed into the port city.

Liborius walked the streets of the port city searching for a bakery, or pistrina. He used his nose as a guide. Though there were not as many pistrinas in a port city, he knew they were common enough because more Romans bought bread than made it. Pistrinas were popular food outlets in towns and cities all over Roman land. It did not take long before the pleasant smells brought him to a large pistrina. As he entered through the street entrance, which he barely spotted with all the carts surrounding it, a worker stopped him at the entrance. He told him that this pistrina did not sell directly to customers, that it only did deliveries. Frustrated, Liborius asked for directions to one that sold bread directly, and the worker gave him directions. Liborius did not want to be long getting the bread and quickened the pace to his destination.

"Alms," cried a beggar on the street. Liborius was not paying much attention and nearly jumped. As his heart stopped racing, he noticed the man who called out. The beggar was thin and gaunt with a lean face and sunken eyes. He appeared to be middle-aged, and his clothes were practically rags. He was missing part of his right leg below his knee and missing practically every tooth, but somehow he managed a crooked smile. A strange something burned in the man's eyes; it was indescribable. Liborius had a flashing thought of sympathy for him. As he walked past the beggar, the beggar called out "alms" again and touched Liborius's arm as he passed. A chill ran down Liborius's spine, and he quickly pushed onward toward the pistrina.

With little effort, Liborius found what he was looking for. This particular pistrina was huge with two large rooms attached to the main building. One room held a large, donkey-driven mill with a millstone made of basalt lava that ground the flour. The second room was equipped with large ovens rigged with ceiling vents to disperse the smoke. The main building was where the magic of dough-making was done, although not always by hand. Machinery was common in Roman baking. There were special kneading machines, and dough was wound around a horizontal shaft in the bottom of the basin and then pressed between wooden slats in the basin's sides. Only the shaping and stamping with the mark of the bakery were done by hand.

Liborius entered the pistrina, meeting a plump baker whose arms were covered in flour up to his elbows. He purchased the requested bread for his master, Lucius. Three loaves total for Lucius, and Liborius suspected he would share some of the bread.

"Will that be all, my friend?" the baker asked.

Liborius thought for a moment. He reached into his pocket and grabbed the sestertius that Lucius handed him earlier. "Let me have one more loaf," said Liborius. The baker gave him change and handed him the loaf. Liborius had two loaves under each arm as he made his way back to the barracks, but first, he had to make one quick stop.

The beggar was at the same location where Liborius had seen him before. With a warm feeling inside, Liborius handed the man the extra loaf he had purchased, still warm from the pistrina's oven. The beggar cracked a smile with a twist to it, like the smile of a child who is determined not to weep. The beggar thanked him and bellowed out, "God bless you, my friend."

Liborius pondered for a second. "Which God?" he responded.

"Why, the only true God," the beggar quickly replied. "The God of Abraham, the God of Isaac, and the God of Jacob." The names were strange to Liborius.

"My name is Ezra," the beggar continued, "I am a Jew, a tentmaker originally from Judea, the land of the Jews, as it is often referred to, but because of my injury, I am not able to work."

Liborius did not know much about Jews, and he was puzzled over what he could remember. They refused to eat pork, which the Romans loved, and why did they circumcise infant boys? He could not understand why there was no image of their God in the Temple and thought the Sabbath rest was a sign of laziness. In a world of many gods, the idea of having just one seemed strange to him.

Jews had spread from their homeland in Judea across the Mediterranean into three major Jewish communities in Syria, Egypt, and Greece. Practicing a very different religion from their neighbors, Jews had lived in Rome since the second century BC. Julius Caesar and Octavian both supported laws that allowed Jews protection to worship as they chose. Synagogues were classified as schools to get around Roman laws banning secret societies, and the temples were allowed to continue and collect the yearly taxes paid by Jewish men for maintaining them.

Liborius had little time to linger, but he was friendly and returned the blessing, "God bless you, too."

Ezra smiled. "My friend, you have shown love; love really does have power. It can reach places the sun can't and warm the very soul."

Liborius let the words sink in. He had never heard love described that way. Lingering for a moment in his thoughts, he shifted the remaining loaves in his arms. Remembering his need for haste, Liobrius spoke abruptly. "Goodbye. I must be on my way." Turning away, Liborius sped off toward the barracks.

It was near noon when Liborius reached the barracks and set to work preparing a meal for Lucius. He was a little late returning, so he moved quickly. The Romans usually consumed only one meal a day around noontime. In fact, eating more than once a day was considered a form of gluttony. The meal today was the coveted bread Liborius had acquired, served along with fresh fish and vegetables. Liborius had just finished putting the meal out and was pouring the wine. He was about to call Lucius in when his master appeared.

"Pour yourself some and join me in this meal. I have something I wish to discuss with you," remarked Lucius. Liborius poured another cup of wine, made a plate for himself, and took a seat.

Lucius's mouth watered the moment he noticed the bread. Grabbing a loaf, he tore it in half, one-half for himself and the other for Liborius. He then devoured his food rapidly, stuffing his mouth too full. After a large sip of wine to wash the meal down, he looked up at Liborius.

"I could not help but see your eyes light up when you looked at the flyer this morning," Lucius said. "Rowing for your freedom. We do need every man available to rid us of Sextus's fleet, but is this something you truly want?"

Liborius just about turned white as the meaning of Lucius's words sank in. His thoughts raced. Liborius had a good life here with Lucius and was treated well. He would actually miss the Legion. The thoughts and emotions trundled through his head like a chariot, with no intention of stopping. After what felt like an eternity, he spoke.

"Master, I truly want this," Liborius croaked out.

"Then go," Lucius declared with a smile. Liborius felt relief at that moment and could not help a tear from escaping his eye. Both men finished their meal in silence.

After the meal, Liborius cleaned up and then was sent out with the soldiers to finish handing out the flyers that were left from earlier in the day. When he completed the task, it was late and getting dark. Slowly, weariness crept into his arms and legs, and after a big stretch, he went to bed. The long minutes dragged into even longer hours, but sleep did not come. As he lay on his bed, he was in deep thought. He truly did not understand what freedom would bring him. Was he sure what he would do after his freedom? Did he make the best decision? He was determined to make something of himself. For years, he had dreamed of joining the army. The training would be rigorous, but if he served a mandatory 25 years, he would gain his citizenship. He would receive three gold coins upon enrolling and the opportunity to build wealth when the army plundered. His mind raced all night, and it turned into serious anxiety without much sleep.

Liborius arrived in the morning, reporting to Lucius after his restless sleep, and discovered the morning orders were about him. Legionnaires would escort him to the rowers' recruitment assembly at the docks. A dozen men were selected from the legionnaires who Liborius was the most familiar with and wanted to say farewell to. Lucius would also join the group that was turning into an honor guard. It was a beautiful, sunny day, and the warmth of the sun felt good. The possessions he carried did not weigh Liborius down. A simple blanket wrapped around a hollowed ram's horn he would use for drinking, and a small clay vessel filled with olive oil and a wooden bowl with matching utensils were for eating. The olive oil he would use to nourish his hair and moisturize his skin. As the group marched, Liborius's mind still grappled with his thoughts from the previous night, but after a good distance, he became mostly excited. Lucius walked by his side but was silent during the walk.

The smell of the sea air alerted the group that they were close to the docks. The cool breeze stole warmth, giving them the taste and smell of brine. The group halted above a small hill looking down at the docks. The fleet being assembled to destroy the Sextus stronghold in Sicily was simply magnificent. Hundreds of warships called triremes filled the port. The bronze rostrum designed for ramming shined brightly in the sun. The triremes were decorated at the prow and stern. At the head of the ship was either a wolf, a wild boar, or a lion. The triremes also held the signature rear archer's tower, and many had weapons of throw called a ballistae. The group traveled down the hill and approached an assembly tent for new rowers joining the fleet. The legionnaires bid their farewells one by one with many giving Liborius an embrace or pat on the back. Then it was Lucius's turn to say goodbye. The tough veteran fought hard to hold back a tear.

"Good luck, Liborius. You have served me well," Lucius spoke. "If we ever meet again, I shall call you friend. Thank you for everything. I hope you live a life of happiness."

He embraced Liborius, not holding back his tears. Lucius then departed with his legionnaires back to the barracks. Liborius could hear them break into song at a distance, and he caught some of the lyrics.

Aquila de prioribus surrexit ad X honorem.
Nec hostis nos vincere posse, ubi res nulla missa est.
Ita eleves ferrum inferre iacula.
Certa victoria sanguine nostro obtulit.
Ut sacrificemus aquilae gloria Caesaris honoribus.

Ut semper Romanus vincat.
Et facta est aquila quoniam in aeternum laudabiliter
cantu proferuntur.
Nunc nos adepto de modo ante vos adepto
amputentur.

The eagle has risen for the honor of the Tenth.
No enemy can defeat us no matter where sent.
So raise your swords and javelins and push forward.
Victory is assured with our blood offered.
We sacrifice for the Eagle's glory and Caesar's honor.
May the Roman Empire forever conquer.
For eternity the deeds of the Eagle will be sung.
Now get out of our way before you get stung.

CHAPTER X

HERO

Before long, Liborius was on board a Roman trireme decorated with a wolf at its head. The bronze rostrum at the bow was a mere artistic extension, losing any military use, unlike the Greeks who still favored ramming. The Romans favored the superiority of the infantry to make the difference in collision fighting. The Roman triremes could accommodate 170 rowers, along with approximately 50 infantry. The infantry was made up of legionnaires experienced in battle. The ship was adjusted to the Roman military standards with a complete bridge, giving more room for fighters. Designed to travel at high speeds, the ship required a high oar-to-gear ratio, which is the ratio of the outside length of an oar to the inside length, and, above all, they needed skilled rowers. The port that housed the oarsmen was small and cramped. Due to the layout of the ship, rowers were unable to see the water and were forced to row blindly, so coordinating the rowing required considerable skill and practice.

Immediately, Liborius started his rigorous training as an oarsman. Two superintendents, or toicharchoi, who were in charge of the rowers instructed on each side of the ship. Liborius listened intently as a piper, or auletes, gave the rowers' rhythm. The piper's melody instructed the men on how hard to row. Liborius wished he did not see the clepsydra, or water clock, that measured reliefs and watches from his seat. The clock seemed to mock him and make him feel like his work was endless. Sweat droplets on his skin began to run down his face and limbs, splashing onto the floor. Beads as salty as tears ran onto his lips. By the time he was done with a shift, he was so wet that his clothes needed wringing out, and his hair was plastered to his scalp. After a long day of rowing, the ship's crew worked to pull the ship up from the water during the night. If the ship was left in the sea too long, it could become waterlogged. The use of light woods meant that this was possible, but it did require a good use of muscle. After the first day of rowing, Liborius had never felt such pain.

His muscles twinged as he took them to near failure. He felt as if he had been beaten in a brawl. His muscles hurt even to the touch. As the long days transpired, the pain began to go away. He was fed well since the fleet was still at port, and he was given plenty of fresh water. He could eat as much polta (a thick soup made of wild grains), legumes, and, when available, meat as he wanted. At night, exhausted, he would go to a tent on shore prepared for the rowers. They had no carts to sleep in, only a large blanket for each man to wrap himself and lie on the ground. The tent was typically quiet because the rowers did not converse much, lacking the energy to stay awake. The silence was like a restorative draft after the rush of the day.

More than just a good crew determined the distance a trireme could cover in a given day, and a lot depended on the weather and water conditions. On a good day, the oarsmen rowed up to eight hours and could propel the ship up to 100 kilometers. Regardless of the weather conditions, they rowed. Liborius could be tossed high from a surging wave, tilted wildly one way and then another. The job of a rower was savage and harsh. It had been one hell of a rough day after another. Liborius did not regret his decision but had no idea how hard he would have to work for his freedom. Happiness seemed so far away, yet he glimpsed the end of his labor when he heard rumors that the fleet would be lining up soon for battle. Sheaves of arrows and armfuls of javelins were carried on deck, along with stones for the artillery.

On September 3, 36 BC, 300 ships of Sextus Pompey's fleet were lined up along the northeast coastline of Sicily, facing north. It was a beautiful day with only a few white, fluffy clouds that married a beautiful blue sky. Behind the ships stood the port city of Naulochus. Octavian had 300 ships under the command of his good friend Admiral Marcus Agrippa. They were lined up directly across from Sextus's fleet. A tremendous sea battle was about to begin. Sextus had all but lost the land battle for Sicily, so his only chance for victory was to destroy Agrippa, who had never fought a sea battle. Sextus believed he had the upper hand. As the ships approached, they launched an artillery barrage at each other. What an amazing scene as hundreds of projectiles flew through the air, some of them flaming. As the fleet drew closer, Agrippa unleashed a secret weapon called the harpax. This Roman catapult-shot grapnel allowed an enemy vessel to be harpooned and then winched alongside for boarding.

The trireme that Liborius sailed on shot the harpax into an approaching vessel. They winched slowly alongside the enemy vessel. The bridge was lowered, and 50 infantry on board grouped together to attack the Sextus rebels. The infantrymen were eager to engage and launched the assault too early. The bridge was not completely attached, and a large gap opened between the ships. The men charged and tried to jump the gap, but many brave soldiers fell into the water. The infantry, now smaller in number, fought desperately to take the other ship. The attack was bloody, and they began to slowly lose the effort. The gap between the ships now narrowed, making it easier to go back and forth. A few enemy soldiers fought their way onto the trireme. The trireme infantry were not on board to defend the ship, but the brave archers on board did the best they could. The shouts and sounds of battle could be heard by the rowers below deck. The rowers were petrified. They could be slaughtered by sword or go down with the ship.

Liborius, no stranger to the sounds of battle, quickly left his seat and headed to the top deck. Wasting no time, he grabbed a gladius from a fallen combatant on deck and charged the enemy. A few rowers joined him without sword but were quickly cut down. Liborius fought for his life, stabbing as quickly as he could. The first enemy soldier overstruck high; Liborius ducked, stabbed the man in the neck, and then moved on to the next man, stabbing him in the gut. He continued on to the last man but stumbled as he lost his balance from a pool of blood, falling to the deck and dropping his sword. The attacker raised his sword in a vicious snarl to finish Liborius, but in a flash, an arrow struck the attacker in the back. With a groan, his attacker collapsed. The archer helped Liborius up and handed him the sword that Liborius dropped. Liborius scanned the ship for more attackers but found had none. He then viewed the carnage on the enemy ship. The triremes infantry was slowly winning but at great cost. Liborius was not about to join the slaughter of battle on the other ship but stood on guard for any enemy who tried to come aboard. Eventually, the battle ended, and the few remaining infantry returned to the ship. Liborius was praised for his heroism and received many a handshake. The victorious trireme released the enemy vessel, but with depleted manpower, they were unable to use the harpax again and focus solely on their artillery use.

The new tactic of using the harpax quickly led to a massacre of Sextus's fleet. Marcus Agrippa lost three ships, while 28 of Sextus's ships sank, 17 fled, and the others were burned or captured. The defeat of Sextus at the battle of Naulochus marked the end of the Pompeian resistance to the Second Triumvirate. No longer a threat, Sextus fled with seven ships to Messina on the island of Sicily and eventually made it to the East where he was defeated in 35 BC by Mark Antony. He fled to Asia Minor but was captured and executed by the Roman general Marcus Titius. The triumvirate continued to live on, and Octavian personally returned to effectively rule Italy, Sardinia, and Corsica after the fighting ended. Antony oversaw the eastern provinces and Gaul, while Lepidus directed affairs in North Africa.

For his bravery, Liborius was awarded the armilla, a type of armband worn on the wrist. He would not receive a gold one as was customary because of his current slave status. Instead, he received a silver one freely. This reward was given based on a president of a former slave who was awarded a gold armillae. However, he was denied the honor because a general disagreed with his rank. The slave received a silver armillae instead. The soldier's immediate commander was determined to see his deeds rewarded and gave gold coins instead, an offer the soldier refused. Shamed into action, the general at last presented him with a silver armilla for proper acknowledgment of his military deeds. With the defeat of Sextus, the rowers were released from service, and Liborius was given his freedom from slavery. The long-awaited dream was his. He searched the depths of his heart for his next move. In the end, he made up his mind to join the army. Joining the legions was just too tempting a prospect, and it was all that he really knew.

CHAPTER XI

NEW RECRUIT

W hen the dilectus came around to recruit for the army, Liborius jumped at the chance. The application was actually relatively easy. You had to be past puberty, and you had to be fit and strong. The months of rowing and good eating had helped Liborius become quite robust and made it easy for him to qualify. He would start as a common tirone, or tiro for short. This was the absolute lowest rank possible in the Roman Army. Tiros were not allowed true shields or swords; they trained with wooden facsimiles deliberately much heavier than those they used in battle. Tirones could expect to spend up to six months in training before they graduated to the rank of gregarius and were sent out into the field. Real swords, shields, and armor were provided by the state, but if you lost them or they were broken, the damages came out of your pay.

Besides the gladius, a recruit was trained in the use of a javelin, also called a pilla, used primarily for stabbing and throwing. This heavy weapon with a large barbed head attached was designed to punch through an opponent's shield and skewer him. If it missed the body, it would break off and lodge in his shield, making it heavier until the Roman grabbed his second javelin and tried again. This spear was the primary weapon to slow down the enemy, and the gladius, a thrusting weapon, did the final killing. Each soldier also carried a large shield about four feet high and two feet wide. Secured to the left arm, it was constructed of layered wood covered in thick leather and typically weighed more than 20 pounds. This hefty shield provided great protection but was also useful as an offensive weapon to knock opponents to the ground. New recruits learned how to use weapons and shields, but their primary lesson was discipline, keeping a level head, and staying in the proper rank and file. Hours of training were spent learning to advance across a battlefield and shift as needed.

After just a few weeks, the ragtag men marched as a cohesive unit. Their legs moved in expert timing, keeping in time to an unheard beat. In a few months more, should they survive, they would be competent in the field, and any fear in their hearts would be replaced with the courage of a warrior. The drill instructors constantly yelled, losing their voices inevitably, especially during the first phase of training when orders were constantly barked.

Sweat dripped from Liborius's forehead, and his muscles ached from holding a heavy shield over his head. His training unit was practicing the important tortoise formation drill. The defensive formation was so strong that it doubled as a bridge that Roman soldiers used as a portable stepladder so their comrades could stand on it to climb over low walls and shoot arrows. The men in front held shields out, tightly interlocking together, while the men behind held their shields up, forming a protective shell over the top of the men. They held this tight formation as they marched slowly forward. Then a shrill sound from a trumpet pierced their ears. The formation immediately broke, and the men charged, screaming at the top of their lungs with swords drawn. They moved with great speed. One man tripped on a stone and fell on his back with the wind knocked out of him. The men continued the charge until another sound of a trumpet bellowed out. The men moved to a quick step and then re-formed into a tight column. They would repeat the drill until it was performed effortlessly.

The new recruits also had to learn the wedge, sometimes referred to as a flying wedge, an offensive-based military formation. The wedge was designed to cut through enemy lines and confuse enemy cavalry. It had soldiers lining up in the shape of a pointed triangle and charging directly at and through the enemy. The weapon carried by those in the wedge formation was a gladius. The advantage of the wedge was that it offered a narrow point for piercing enemy formations and concentrated the leaders at the front. Liborius was selected for the honor of leading the formation. Like a flight of cranes, the formation moved toward another training unit playing the enemy. The wedge struck hard, and using wooden swords, they brutally attacked the opposition. Train as you fight, the instructors taught them. The only rule for them was not to strike the head. The wedge was sure to win, but the defenders put up a good fight. After many bruises, the wedge cleared through the defenders. Liborius felt a sense of pride. There was no doubt that the wedge would be victorious, but he reveled in the moment of command, if only for a short while.

Liborius's final task in order to graduate was a 20-mile march to be completed in five hours carrying a full pack of weapons, shield, food rations, a cooking pot, a short spade, and a personal kit. After successfully completing the exhausting march, Liborius was officially part of the Roman Army and promoted to gregarius. He had not been assigned to a particular legion yet, so he petitioned in an attempt to rejoin the Tenth, which was marching in a few months to join Mark Antony in the Parthian campaign. Antony was determined to carry out the invasion of Parthian territory as Caesar had planned before his untimely death. The commander of the training was glad to send the petition and sent it along with a letter supporting Liborius's attempt to join the Tenth. Liborius, with his silver armilla, had performed well in his training and demonstrated great skill. Even with Liborius's great performance, it would be a long shot. He would not be assigned until the letter came back from the Tenth with the response to his request.

There is a kind of waiting that feels like a gentle, onshore breeze caressing salty stones. There is a sense of calmness of things expected. Then there is the kind that feels like the tip of a gladius in your gut, and your head has taken a beating with a big plank of wood. As Liborius waited for the decision, it was the latter. Days turned into weeks and still no answer from the Tenth. Then, on an auspicious morning, the commander of the training requested Liborius's presence immediately. The commander was holding a letter that Liborius guessed was from the Tenth. As the commander opened the letter, Liborius trembled with anticipation.

Reading the letter, the commander's eyes bulged, and he smiled. "Liborius, you will be marching with the Tenth. You will depart immediately. The Tenth is moving out soon. The gods must favor you. Simply astonishing!" Liborius thanked the commander and swiftly departed. He would be walking by foot on the road to Brundisium. The Tenth was departing soon from Brundisium, and they would not wait for a new recruit.

CHAPTER XII

PROVE YOURSELF IN BATTLE

L ike the First Triumvirate, the Second Triumvirate was also unstable and could not withstand the jealousies and greed of its builders. Antony detested Octavian and spent most of his time in the East, while Lepidus felt like a side note to his counterparts. During the campaign against Sextus Pompey, Lepidus had raised a large army with a formidable navy and had success in his invasion of Sicily, capturing a good amount of territory. However, he felt that Octavian was treating him as an outsider, not as a partner. That led to a bad decision that gave Octavian the excuse he needed to remove Lepidus from power. After the defeat of Sextus Pompey, Lepidus continued to station his army in Sicily and argued that Sicily should be part of his territories, which had originally been spelled out under the Second Triumvirate. Octavian accused Lepidus of supplanting the Roman people and inciting rebellion. Embarrassingly, Lepidus's army in Sicily defected to Octavian, and Lepidus was forced to submit to Octavian. Lepidus was stripped of all his titles except that of Pontifex Maximus and was sent into exile at Circeii.

In order to provide booty and spoils for his troops and tout his reputation as a military commander, Octavian pursued a war in Illyricum, modern-day northern Albania, Montenegro, Bosnia, Herzegovina, and coastal Croatia, to bring it under Roman control. Meanwhile, Antony made war against the Parthian Empire, modern-day Iran. Caesar had desired to campaign against Parthia and take its vast wealth, but he never got the chance. However, Antony was over-confident and went to war hastily; he was forced to retreat, losing more than a quarter of his military strength in the course of defeat.

In 41 BC, Mark Antony collected support against the Parthians and ordered Cleopatra to Tarsus to meet him and answer questions about her loyalty. During the Roman Civil War, she was rumored to have given money to Cassius, who plotted against Caesar. It seems that, in fact, Antony wanted Cleopatra's promise to support his intended war against the Parthians. Antony was willing to overlook a lot to defeat the Parthians. Cleopatra reportedly arrived in a grand state on a gold-encrusted royal barge. Antony expected Cleopatra to come to his palace, but Cleopatra, fearing for her life, made Antony meet her on her barge that was docked. Antony was so charmed that he began an affair with her almost immediately. The relationship was so strong that he moved to Cleopatra's home in Alexander, but he did not marry her. Antony, in order to cement an alliance with Octavian, married Octavian's sister, Octavia.

To protect herself and Caesarion, her son by Julius Caesar, Cleopatra had Antony order the death of her sister, Arsinoe, who had been banished to the Temple of Artemis for her role in leading the Siege of Alexandria during the time Caesar was engaged in the civil war between himself and the armies of the Roman Senate. In 44 BC, Antony visited Alexandria again en route to make war against the Parthians, and from that point on, he stayed with Cleopatra at her home in Alexandria. On December 25, 40 BC, Cleopatra gave birth to her first children with Antony. The twins were named Alexander Helios and Cleopatra Selene II. He most likely ignored advice and married

Cleopatra even though he was already married to Octavian's sister. Although he married Cleopatra, according to the Egyptian custom, the marriage was illegal under Roman law. Antony did not care; he was severing his ties with Rome and Octavian. He would acquire land not for Rome but for his own empire. He sought out the revived empire of Alexander the Great. Antony had a final child with Cleopatra, named Ptolemy Philadelphus. Unfortunately for him, Antony's relationship with Cleopatra offended more than just Octavian, and many Romans viewed the act as treason. When the Triumvirates' second term expired in 33 BC, Antony continued to use the title of triumvir, but Octavian stopped using the title to distance himself from Antony.

After Antony's failed war with Parthia, he turned his attention to Armenia. The Tenth Legion was being transferred to the East to bolster Antony's war against the Parthian Empire and his invasion of Armenia. Liborius arrived at the last possible moment to join the Legion just prior to their departure to the East. He had walked many miles, which took several days, to meet the Legion at the heel of Italy in Brundisium on the Adriatic coast. Stopping only to make a quick camp to sleep on the side of the road, Liborius followed the Appian Way. This most famous and important of Roman roads ran more than 200 miles south from Rome and ended in Brundisium. The Romans built their roads straight as an arrow across the landscape. The roads were a sermon in stone to the world that Romans do not yield. It was a wonderful feeling for Liborius to be free and go as he pleased. The trip was grueling, but he was in great physical condition. When weariness crept into his legs, he would hum a marching song and push forward, focusing on his destination. At last, he came to the encampment of the Tenth Legion and navigated his way immediately to the officers' tents to check in.

On his way to the officers' tents, Lucius spotted Liborius. Lucius was jubilant and could not believe his eyes. Lucius stopped Liborius and promptly gave him a huge bear hug. "We have some catching up to do, my fellow legionnaire," he grinned. "I see a silver armilla on your wrist. Primo! I will make arrangements for you to be under my command. Join me in my tent after you pick up your equipment and secure it in your quarters. We have a lot to talk about." His eyes hinted of amusement as if he knew something Liborius didn't know.

Liborius left Lucius and went straight off to check in at the command tent and then off to the supply area, receiving his state equipment, including two javelins, a shield, and a shovel. Then he was given his own gladius, one of the most prized possessions of a Roman foot soldier. He was also given a small chest to keep his possessions in and hopefully some future booty. The last place he visited was the ration tent where he was handed a sack of grain, meat jerky, vegetables, and a small bag of salt. Typically, rations were only given out on the first of the month, always deducted from a soldier's pay to prevent, it was said, the disciplined legionnaire from overeating and drinking.

Liborius searched for an open place in the legionnaires' quarters under Lucius's command. The legionnaires' quarters were located in eight 10-foot by 10-foot tents, called a contubernium. The contubernium was a squad who lived and worked together, especially with the task of food preparation. They worked as a team using a mill to make their own grain and create their own bread, a blackish bread made from coarse grain and baked over a campfire. The finer grained white bread went to the officers. Each contubernium also included a pack mule that carried the tent, tent poles, various tools, cooking utensils, and one slave.

Liborius found an opening in one of the tents and placed his equipment there. Then he introduced himself briefly to the men there. Their eyes were hardened from many a battle, and they viewed Liborius suspiciously. A few of them recognized Liborius from his service to Lucius, but one look at the silver armilla and they welcomed him like a brother. All the men shook Liborius's hand and introduced themselves. After introductions, the men told Liborius how they looked forward to the upcoming campaign and how it promised great opportunity for spoils. The men inquired about the silver armilla, and Liborius told them how he earned it. The men were impressed with the story, and Liborius hoped he could live up to their expectations. With introductions completed, Liborius packed away his equipment and arranged his sleeping area. Leaving his quarters, he took a short walk to see Lucius.

"Liborius, we need a new aquilifer to bear the Legion's Eagle Standard. I hope you are up for the task. I know you and trust you. Survive the upcoming battle, and the position is yours." Liborius's jaw dropped as he heard the words. There was no greater honor than bearing the Legion's standard.

As Liborius's mind raced, he stuttered, "I won't let you down."

"I know you won't," Lucius said. "Now share a drink with me."

Lucius poured Liborius a cup of posca, a watered-down sour wine popular among the common soldiers. Liborius filled Lucius in on his adventures after leaving the service of his former master. They talked late into the night and at times got a bit tipsy. Eventually, Liborius departed Lucius's tent and returned to his contubernium. As he lay down next to his comrades, he thought to himself how grateful he was. Maybe he should thank some deity for having such luck, but whom should he thank? "Well, to whichever deity that helped me, I thank you," he whispered. He thought for a moment and then remembered the hungry Jew he had given bread to. Not to offend and just in case, he whispered, "Thank you, God."

It was not long before the Tenth Legion, along with three other legions of Mark Antony, were deployed against King Artavasdes's army in Armenia. The Tenth led the center and quickly fell into formation. They marched in a tight formation with shields locked together. On the left and right side of the army, they were supported by Gaulic auxiliaries to counter the enemy's cavalry units. After a terrifying burst of arrows and ballista bolts, the army marched at a slow, steady pace toward the enemy. They marched in strictly observed silence and restraint. The Tenth hurled their javelins with two volleys and then charged into the Armenian army with a thunderous battle cry while keeping their solid formation. The cavalry quickly disappeared out of sight to battle their counterparts. The veteran Tenth, the most beloved of Caesar's legions, fought the enemy unmercifully. Liborius, as was the custom with a new recruit, fought in the front ranks. It was better to lose a green newbie than lose a veteran legionnaire. The front rank held tightly together and hit the enemy hard, face-to-face.

Liborius used his heavy shield as much as a weapon, bashing the enemy and then quickly stabbing at his enemies' abdomens with his gladius. His heart pounded as he pushed forward. One thing was sure, it was going to be a very painful day. With luck, Liborius would escape harm with only a few cuts and bruises. The Armenian army was not putting up much of a fight, and they easily gave way to the legions. After Liborius was covered mostly with enemy blood and had reached his physical limit, he rotated out of position so a fresh soldier could take his place. The legion was an effective killing machine, crushing the enemy's center. Just as the Armenian army's center was finished, the Tenth's auxiliary cavalry hit the enemy from behind, having already defeated their cavalry. The ensuing victory was more of a massacre. Drawing deep, ragged breaths, Liborius shouted victory cries as loudly as he could with his fellow legionnaires. The battle was over before it ever started, and Mark Antony took control of Armenia.

The sun was many hours below the horizon, and Liborius ached from head to foot after hours of fighting. He lay in his contubernium tent, exhausted. All the men were tired, but they shared stories from the day's battle under the glow of candlelight. Suddenly, Lucius entered the tent holding the Eagle Standard.

"Good job, men. You surely gave them a whipping!" He spoke proudly. Taking off his helmet, he set it beside the candle. "Liborius, it is a great honor for me to give you the Eagle Standard to carry. I know you will not fail to protect it. It was my privilege years ago, and now it is yours." Liborius took the Eagle Standard, his eyes fiercely bright with pride, and held it up. The men erupted in applause and cheers, and Lucius waited patiently until the men settled down. "Now get some rest. You've all earned it." Lucius picked up his helmet from beside the candle and walked out of the tent.

CHAPTER XIII
WAR IS HELL

Mark Antony was now practically an emperor in the East. Cleopatra and Caesarion were crowned co-rulers of Egypt and Cyprus at Alexandria in late 34 BC. After Antony's conquest of Armenia, the children of Cleopatra and Antony were given territory to rule, and Antony gave Cleopatra the title Queen of Kings. Her enemies in Rome began to truly fear that Cleopatra was planning a war of revenge that was to array all the East against Rome and that she would establish herself as empress of the world at Rome. Her son, Caesarion, was elevated to co-regency with Cleopatra and was also given many titles, including god, son of god, and king of kings, and he was depicted as the Egyptian deity Horus. Egyptians already thought that Cleopatra was a goddess— the reincarnation of the goddess Isis.

Relations between Antony and Octavian had been disintegrating for several years, and they finally broke down completely in 33 BC. To drum up support, Octavian illegally obtained Antony's will. He forced the priestesses of the temple of Vesta in Rome to surrender Antony's will and had it read out loud in the Senate. On July 32 BC, it was exposed to the Roman public. The will exposed promises that gave legacies to Antony's children by Cleopatra and left instructions for shipping his body to Alexandria for burial. Among the worst of Antony's offenses was that the true heir of Caesar would be Caesarion, not Octavian. Octavian convinced the frightened Senate to levy war against the Egyptian Queen Cleopatra. Antony, her lover and ally, betrayed the Roman government and joined the war on Cleopatra's side. The stage was set for a final Roman civil war. Antony and Octavian prepared their legions for war. The legions in the East, including the Tenth Legion, stayed loyal to Antony.

By mid-summer of 31 BC, Antony maneuvered his army into Greece, and Octavian soon followed. Octavian brought with him one of his closest friends, Marcus Agrippa, who previously won victory against Sextus. Although the ground forces were equal, Octavian's fleet, though smaller, had maneuverable ships called libunas filled with experienced sailors. Octavian wanted to battle Antony by sea where his experienced sailors could dominate. The classic Roman ships of Antony, triremes, and the much larger quinqueremes were primarily designed to board enemy ships that had been hooked close by means of iron grapnels. Antony had the same type of ships Agrippa used to destroy Sextus decisively years ago. In contrast, Octavian had libuna-type ships that were used for raiding and patrols that could ram, rain arrows, and fire catapults large enough to decapitate a man.

As the summer ended and autumn began to set in, both Octavian and Antony avoided battle and focused on wearing down the other. This strategy worked well for Octavian as morale sank, and many abandoned Antony's cause. With Antony's army shrinking, he decided to move his fleet to Actium in western Greece to strike against Octavian's navy and army at camp while he was still able.

Antony held a war meeting in his command tent with all his legion commanders and officers. They included the workhorse of the army, the Centurions. The legionary representatives filed into the tent with the Tenth's representatives, including Lucius, entering last.

Antony wasted no time speaking to the men: "Our fleet in Actium along with Cleopatra's navy is ready to crush Octavian. It is by sea we will earn victory here!"

The men shuffled in silence, and Lucius, a veteran of countless battles, spoke up. "Let us destroy Octavian on land. We are eager to fight and able to maneuver on any ground but not on ships. Destroy Octavian's army with the Tenth in the center and let's end this war."

Antony sighed loudly and retorted, "None is your equal fighting on land or at sea. I will put the most skilled and experienced soldiers on board, we cannot lose!"

Silently, the officers strongly agreed with what Lucius had said, but they held their tongues. Many in sympathy with Lucius's feelings dropped their gaze.

Antony continued. "We will destroy Octavian at sea, and then we will continue toward Rome and finish this war. Now, go to your men and prepare them. We will attack soon." Then Antony muttered, "I will lead you to victory," and abruptly departed the tent. The representatives remained for a little while. Some argued among themselves, but most walked out with heads down, believing Lucius was correct.

Lucius returned to his tent. He was not happy, but he had his orders. He sent immediately for his most seasoned veterans and then instructed them to be ready to board ships when the command came. Liborius was anguished at not having been selected. The newly promoted aquilifer spoke to Lucius in private and begged to go with the veterans.

"The Eagle Standard will stay on land, my friend," Lucius spoke with a forced smile. "I will join you after the battle, and we will march the eagle to Rome." Calming himself with an effort, Liborius accepted the decision. When the call came, the veterans loaded on board. Queasiness settled in Liborius's stomach when he heard that most of the officers disagreed on the battle strategy. The feeling of anxiety grew in him. For a while he tried to shrug it off. The feeling not only persisted but grew stronger.

On September 2, 31 BC, Antony moved his large ships through the strait and into the open sea. There, Octavian's light and maneuverable liburnian ships drew in battle formation against Antony's warships. Cleopatra's ships stayed behind Antony's navy. What was unknown to Antony was that one of his former generals had delivered Antony's battle plan to Octavian. Antony had hoped to use his biggest ships to drive back the north end of his line, but Octavian's entire fleet stayed carefully out of range. In the late afternoon, Antony extended his line out from the protection of the shore and finally engaged the enemy. Agrippa commanded Octavian's fleet, armed with Antony's battle plan and more maneuverable ships. The armies of Octavian and Antony watched as Antony's larger navy was destroyed. Cleopatra was at the battle with a small fleet, but after seeing Antony's destruction, she made a run for the open sea without firing a shot, leaving Antony to fend for himself. As a hole opened in Agrippa's blockade, she escaped, followed by Antony's command ship. Antony retreated and fled toward Alexandria. By the end of the day, Antony's entire fleet lay at the bottom of the sea.

Liborius watched in horror from shore as Antony's fleet was destroyed. Tears ran down his face at the loss of Lucius and the many veterans of the Tenth Legion. There was more than just sadness as Antony's remaining army watched the fleet sink, their knuckles turning white from clenching their fists too hard and their faces reddening with suppressed rage. The commanders of Antony's land army, who were ordered to follow him to Asia, promptly surrendered their legions without a fight. Even though Octavian wanted to immediately pursue Antony and Cleopatra, he needed to attend to the army.

Many of the veterans were tired of war and wanted to retire and return to private life. Most of those legionnaires could trace their service to Julius Caesar. Octavian allowed many of his longest serving veterans the equivalent of almost 10 legions to retire. The Tenth Legion joined Octavian but was completely stripped of most of the veterans. Lucius's former position of centurion was given to Survius Felix, who previously held the position of optio centuria, command of the rear guard and second in command under a centurion. Felix chose to promote Liborius to his former position of optio. Felix handed him his badge of office, a wooden staff with a metal ball at the end, often used to back his orders. He also handed Liborius his old helmet in order to be visible in action. The optio helmet had black and white plumes mounted fore and aft, with the tail hanging at the rear of the helmet. Liborius was grateful for the promotion and took to liking Felix right away.

Felix had experience leading troops in battle. His eyes were a brown as rich as the earth's soil. Those deep pools seized the burden of a thousand untold stories. On the other side of his brown orbs was a mischievous glint that blazed with humor and gaiety that never seemed to escape. It was Felix who gave the news that Lucius's will had been read. Felix explained that Lucius had made Liborius his heir as an adopted son at his death. This made Liborius instantly wealthy. Lucius had been saving his money and spoils for many years for the family he never had. Also, because Lucius had been granted Roman citizenship for acts of valor, the citizenship passed on to his adopted son, Liborius. Liborius would have given it all up to have Lucius back. In his mind, Lucius was his only family, in a sense the only father figure Liborius had ever known since he had been taken from his family in Gaul at such a young age so many years ago. Liborius was grateful that Lucius had thought him so worthy of this inheritance. He vowed to himself to be a good steward of the wealth and not be conned into handing it over to anyone. *I'm going to do something with it that would make Lucius proud,* he thought to himself.

The fall made it to winter, and the Tenth was gradually resupplied with new men. The Tenth was still needed. Antony was defeated, but he was still holed up in Alexandria with Cleopatra. Weeks before, the mud had frozen solid, as hard as any rock. Now, the ground lay covered in a blanket of virgin white, and the earthen brown would not be seen until the spring thaw. The wintry cold howled through the desolate camp that was covered with fluffy snow. They could feel the heavy air as their lungs filled with sharp cold each time they breathed in. The bleak, gray clouds overhead reflected perfectly the Tenth's gloomy mood.

CHAPTER XIV
NEW BEGINNING

SPQR

The frost in its wintry song reflected the brilliance of the sunshine in every direction. The ice-cold wind blew hard as Liborius made his way through camp. Frosted air pushed its way into his lungs and bit his eyes. Liborius's first act as optio was to give the noble duty of carrying the Eagle Standard to a worthy man to bear. Unfortunately, there were not many veterans remaining to choose from. At last, he chose the sole remaining legionnaire in his previous contubernium. All the other veterans had elected to retire.

The gray-haired veteran's name was Brutus. Brutus trembled with enthusiasm as he took the standard. He held it close. "I promise to protect the Eagle with my life."

Liborius looked him directly in his eyes. "I know you will, Brutus, and thanks for sticking around."

Brutus grinned. "My pleasure, optio. Who else will show the men how to march with the Tenth? Not just any soldier worth his salt makes blood for the glory of his general."

Liborius patted Brutus's shoulder and departed the warm tent and headed out into the bone-chilling cold. The next act was for

Liborius to review his men and introduce himself. He called them into formation regardless of the frigid temperature. Snow began to fall, fat flakes that dotted the men's uniforms. He looked them over as they stood in formation. The men shifted in the bitter cold. They were surely a motley crew. They looked like Roman soldiers and smelled like Roman soldiers, but they had the eyes of foals just learning to walk. They were mostly auxiliary recruits from all over the Roman Empire, fresh out of training. The recruits had Greeks, Gauls, and Middle Easterners represented among them. They were mostly landless poor who found military service attractive.

Liborius addressed them: "Welcome to the Tenth, Caesar's most cherished legion, cherished because we work the hardest and are the first to fight and the last to leave the field." Liborius took a deep breath and sighed. "Great men have fallen for the honor of the Tenth." Just then a powerful gust of stinging wind blew hard, making it difficult for Liborius to continue. "I have no doubt you will honor them with your lips, but also honor them with your actions." He continued hoarsely. "Though we shed our blood for the lives, liberties, and fortunes of the Roman people, our hearts belong to the Tenth. No retreat. No surrender. That is the creed of the Tenth." He dismissed his men and sought the warmth of a fire.

After the winter ended, Octavian resumed the fight with Antony. Instead of attacking Alexandria directly by sea invasion, he traveled by land through Asia. The Tenth Legion began the long march to Egypt for the showdown in Alexandria. They would travel through Greece across the Hellespont and proceed down the Mediterranean coast through Israel and into Egypt. The Tenth marched with several other legions that were eager to finish off Antony. They had marched many miles when they passed through the Kingdom of Judea ruled by Herod the Great. The name Judea was derived from the ancient Kingdom of Judah.

Herod was a close ally of Rome. It was Rome that made it possible for him to be king. His father, Antipater, gave him the governorship of Galilee in 47 BC. After his father's death, Herod feuded with his brother and various Roman factions for control of Antipater's kingdom. In 40 BC, the Parthians, sensing weakness, invaded Syria and Palestine and captured Jerusalem. Herod's brother, his major competition for the throne, was captured and later committed suicide. Herod fled to Rome.

After much turmoil and civil war in Israel, the Romans under General Pompey conquered Jerusalem, the capital of Judea and capital of the Jewish world, in 63 BC. In an effort to keep order over the Judean and Galilean people, Caesar and the Senate installed Herod as King of the Jews, with Judaism officially recognized as a legal religion. Cleopatra, the Egyptian queen, constantly chipped away at some of the most lucrative parts of Herod's kingdom. With Octavian's victory at Actium, which ended Antony and Cleopatra's influence, Herod forged a useful new partnership with Octavian, who saw no reason to look for another puppet.

The army was to take a brief rest for about a week in Judea and then continue nonstop to confront Antony. The Tenth Legion would be staying in the Antonia Fortress built by Herod, and the irony that the fortress was named after Herod's former patron, Antony, did not escape them. The fortress was part of the border wall protecting Jerusalem. King Herod was generous and paid lavishly to entertain the army, most likely to make amends for once supporting Antony. The men would watch games and view plays performed by artists brought in to perform. The Tenth would also entertain themselves in the city, drinking and engaging in all types of debauchery.

Liborius had made many friends in the Tenth. He also held the respect of his rank. Near the fortress by the sheep's gate was the Pool of Bethesda with its five porches. Liborius was curious about the healing powers many attributed to the waters. He put together a small group who wanted to visit the celebrated pool. The party was made up of eight men from various contubernia. They did not wear their armor but brought their gladiuses under their clothing in case they needed them. They made the short journey to the pool early in the morning to avoid the crowds. At the pool, they looked down on ordinary looking water. The pool was used by both Jews and Romans. A small shrine to Asclepius, the Roman god of healing, stood near the pool. Located just outside the city walls, its presence was tolerated by the Jews, who might otherwise have objected to a non-Jewish religious presence in their holy city. The few Jews in the pool area quickly left when they saw the group of Romans.

The men stripped down to their loincloths and entered the pool. The waters remarkably turned red when disturbed. Liborius and the men did not feel any miraculous power from the water and hoped maybe they would feel something after they came out. The men, splashing and laughing, enjoyed the water and thought nothing of the sacredness of the pool. Liborius sat down in the water and watched his men enjoy themselves. Out of the corner of his eye, he noticed a cripple in rags struggling to make it to the water. The man crawled slowly over to the water but could not lift himself into the pool. The men who had come with Liborius did not pay any attention to the man; in fact, they purposely ignored him. Liborius felt an ache in his heart for the man. Before he knew it, he went over to the man, gently lifted him, and carried him into the water. The man's face lit up with pure joy as the water touched him. After a few minutes, Liborius carefully took the man out of the pool. The grateful man looked Liborius in the eye and clasped his hand with both of his. Liborius smiled the universal language of kindness and then watched as the man dragged himself away from the pool. Liborius felt warmth inside and wondered briefly why none of his men had thought to help the man. Gathering the men, he left the pool and headed back to the fortress. No man felt any usefulness from the pool other than the play it provided them. Liborius continued to feel the warmth and strength his actions gave his heart.

Trapped in Egypt with the remnant of their former army, Antony and Cleopatra bided their time awaiting Octavian's arrival.

They reached out to Lucius Pinarius, grandnephew of Caesar by one of his sisters and cousin to Octavian, a commander of four legions in North Africa who had previously supported Antony. Pinarius, in an act of betrayal, had rejected Antony's messengers and had them put to death. He then gave his legions over to Octavian for command. Octavian's and Pinarius's legions planned to arrive at Alexandria and place the entire city under siege. Pinarius's legions would arrive from the west, and Octavian would arrive from the east. Before Octavian arrived, Antony took approximately 10,000 soldiers he had remaining and attacked Pinarius' legions. Unfortunately for Antony, he was unaware that his army was outnumbered almost two to one. Pinarius's legions quickly destroyed what was left of Antony's army, and Antony escaped back to Alexandria just before Octavian arrived. As Octavian approached with his legions to confront Antony in Alexander, what remained of Antony's force surrendered to Octavian. Antony's cause was lost.

Antony was forced to watch as his army and any hopes of dominance in Rome were destroyed by Octavian. In what is considered honorable Roman tradition, Antony, on August 1, 30 BC, committed suicide, falling on his sword. According to the many accounts, however, he was not entirely successful, and with an open wound in his belly was taken to join Cleopatra who had fled to her mausoleum. There, Antony succumbed to his wound and perhaps died in his lover's arms, leaving her alone to face Octavian.

Contrary to popular belief, Cleopatra did not immediately follow Antony in suicide. Instead, in a last act of desperation, Cleopatra begged negotiations with Octavian. She was able to communicate with him and pleaded with Octavian to not kill her son, Caesarion, and in exchange, she would willingly be imprisoned. Octavian had no sympathy for Cleopatra and refused. Instead, Octavian informed Cleopatra that she was to play a role in Octavian's triumph back in Rome. This role was explained to her, and Caesarion was later killed. Octavian may have thought two Caesars were one too many when he ordered the death of Caesarion and Antony's eldest son, who was executed as a possible threat to Rome.

How Cleopatra died is not clear, but it was most likely from a self-induced bite from a venomous snake or from applying a poisonous ointment to her skin. Learning of Cleopatra's death, Octavian may have had mixed feelings. He gave Cleopatra and Antony a public military funeral in Rome. Egypt was annexed and added to the Roman Empire. With the death of Antony and Cleopatra, the final war of the Republic was over, and a new age dawned in Rome. In 27 BC, Octavian was crowned the first emperor of the Roman Empire, and the Senate bestowed upon him the title Augustus.

CHAPTER XV
DON'T FORGET YOUR ROOTS

The era of Augustus's reign was a peaceful and prosperous time in the Roman Empire. In order to keep from making the same mistake his adoptive father had made of seeming to covet power, Octavian was careful not to refer to himself by titles in public but referred to himself as First Citizen, even with the supreme power, giving him absolute control over Rome and her territories. Octavian did not forget the military for making his reign possible. He spent large sums of money turning them into a true, professional army. Since the army was made up of mostly volunteers, Octavian needed to convince young Romans to dedicate their working lives to the army. He even set aside a portion of the Roman treasury to provide financial support and pensions for the troops.

Liborius remained in the army, working with Felix and determined to make the Tenth Legion the pride of the Roman Army. The Tenth was given orders to serve in Judea under King Herod and keep a close eye on the region. They would occupy the Antonia Fortress in Jerusalem where they had stayed briefly before. They marched from Egypt, in no great hurry, to their destination. On the march, a Celtic contingent joined them on the journey. They marched beside the century that Felix and Liborius commanded. Former bodyguards of Cleopatra, they numbered 30. They were to be given as a gift by Octavian to Herod following his victory over Antony. They were fierce warriors who believed their souls were immortal and did not fear death. Death to them was a mere transition phase. It was said the belief was so strong that people could put off repayment of debts to the afterlife. Physically bigger than the Romans, the Celts wielded long, double-edged, iron swords designed for slashing and carried body-length shields painted in reds, greens, and other bright colors, decorated with boars, dragons, and various designs. Despite the heat, they were each equipped with chain mail and well-crafted iron helmets.

Today, the sun was at full blast, and Liborius just wished that someone would turn it down. He was dripping sweat from his head to his toes. The burn from the sun on the marchers didn't go away but instead grew steadily stronger and harder to ignore as the day went on. Looking ahead, he noticed the leader of the Celtic guard struggle as he saw the sun shine brighter than he had ever seen before. He knew little about the warrior except for his name, Aife.

Under Aife's iron helmet peeked out unkempt and dirty, blonde, flowing hair. Aife's consciousness ebbed away with the heat. He took a few blinks from his hazel and honey colored eyes before he landed with a thud. Liborius was at Aife's side quickly, along with husky Celtic warriors. With Liborius's intervention, they managed to carry Aife to one of the few wagons that traveled with them. The wagon supplies were tossed heedlessly to the ground to make room for Aife. His armor was quickly removed, and he was doused with no sparing of water. Aife coughed as his face was soaked, the drops coming together to run into his eyes and drip from his chin. A dazed Aife, a bit embarrassed, tried to lift himself up. He intended to join his men but was ordered to stay in the cart by the medicus vulnerarius who had just arrived on the scene.

"You will stay in here until the Tenth breaks later for camp," the medicus sniffed. "Or will you have me go to the commander?" Aife reluctantly gave in. Liborius quickly had supplies from the wagon dispersed to his men to carry by hand, and they continued the march.

When the Tenth finally made camp for the night, Liborius went to check on Aife. He found Aife in a large tent that Aife shared with his men. Aife was seated on the ground in the center of the tent and appeared to be chanting in Celtic tongue with his men, who were also sitting on the ground. He thought it was Aife, though he was dressed in a strange mask of bright, painted straw. The men became silent as Liborius entered the tent and froze where he was.

Liborius spoke nervously. "How are you feeling, Aife?"

Aife pulled off his mask and turned to Liborius, answering in Roman. "We are celebrating Samhain as best we can far from our island. The veil between the spirits of the departed is at its thinnest today." He motioned for Liborius to be seated. "On this night, the Cailleach, that old hag, comes to strip the leaves from the trees, to quicken the decay of the flesh of the year so that it may feed the new life to come. We also ask her to take the unwanted aspects of our personal year away so these, too, might be transformed." Aife put his mask back on and continued the short ceremony until it ended. He asked Liborius to remain seated, and then, standing up, Aife dismissed his men into the camp.

"No need to check on me." Aife scratched his head trying to remember Liborius's name. "I am fine," he declared.

Liborius smiled. "I can see that, and I am glad to hear it."

Aife raised an eyebrow. "I heard you and your men visited Judea before."

Liborius forthwith told Aife all he knew about Judea and the Jewish people he remembered.

Aife shrugged. "The pay will be good. We are honored to serve. I hear with your slight accent and build you are not fully Roman. Maybe a Celt from Gaul?"

Surprise filled Liborius, and he stood up. He had not shared his full story before and felt relieved as he shared his tale with Aife. Liborius and Aife spoke for a while until Aife's men returned. After introductions, the men treated Liborius like a long-lost brother, sharing stories along with plenty of wine. It was great to hear tales of ancestors and traditions not known to Liborius. Though the men were not from Gaul, they shared blood more similar to Liborius's than that of a Roman. They were from the Catuvellauni tribe who lived in south Britannia linked to Belgic Gaul. Celtic society radiated outward from as far as Britannia, Germainia, and Hispania to the Hellespont. Celts held to tribal loyalties and did not understand a concept such as Rome. Rome had grown from an insignificant village on the Tiber River to a world empire. Liborius attempted to explain Roman life and the rewards of citizenship, but it was too foreign for them to understand. It was getting late, and soon the march would continue to Judea.

Just before Liborius departed the tent, Aife took Liborius aside and whispered, "Don't forget your roots, Liborius, especially tonight. You may not hear your ancestors, but they are always around us." Liborius shifted awkwardly. Aife drew closer. "Do not worry. Even on the darkest night of Samhain, while our minds ponder the departed, if we listen carefully, we can hear the sounds of a heart beating, for soon, time will turn once more."

Liborius returned to his tent that he shared with a canteberium under his command. The men were already asleep as he struggled in the darkness to find his sleep area. He could not shake off his conversation with Aife. Did he forget his roots? What would his Celtic ancestors think of him? What did he believe in so he could make correct decisions in life? Did it even matter? One thought for sure, he was a member of the Roman war machine. There was a long march again tomorrow and work to be done in Judea.

CHAPTER XVI

THE NEW STUDENT

Octavian had forgiven Herod for siding with Antony and let him remain king. With the support of Octavian, Herod's reign was largely a calm one, although he gained a fierce reputation for being oppressive. His relationship with Rome did not oblige him to pay tribute, although he did send handsome gifts. By 30 BC, he had regained control of all the territories that Cleopatra had taken from him. Then, between 23 and 20 BC, with Octavian's blessing, he expanded his realm into northern Galilee and repopulated certain areas with sympathetic settlers. A gifted administrator, he created a new priestly class by abolishing the hereditary qualification for office and establishing a new multicultural aristocracy. He also gave his kingdom a better recognition in the Roman Empire by supporting the Olympics Games and giving lavish gifts to Athens. He restored and reconstructed the Temple of Jerusalem, had a second marriage to a princess from a priestly family of Jewish leaders, and continually pleaded the cause of the Jews of the Diaspora or those in exile to the emperor. His now expanded kingdom comprised Judea,

Samaria, Galilee, Idumea, Batanea, and Peraea, which was approximately the same size of the kingdom of David and Solomon.

Although Herod had exceptional leadership skills, he was extremely disliked by his subjects, the Jews. His attitude toward the Hellenistic Greek dynasty, to which he was related by his first marriage, along with his insolence and cruelty, angered them all the more. He imposed hefty taxes and ruthlessly suppressed any defiance. But it was his policy of embracing Hellenistic culture that most wounded the Jews. Hellenistic projects were built throughout his kingdom with the use of thousands of Jews as forced laborers to move enormous blocks of stone. He ordered the construction of a race track, a theater, and an amphitheater in Jerusalem, and the Jews despised him for it. The Jewish people would never forgive Herod's support of the emperors' cult in the East and his building of pagan temples abroad. The people reluctantly followed under the yoke of Herod, but there was no love between the king and the people. Herod had the support of Octavian's powerful legion to back him up, and he spared no expense on the military that protected his rule. Many fortifications were built, the most famous of which was the fortress of Masada along the Dead Sea and the Antonia Fortress in Jerusalem.

The Tenth Legion was now stationed in Jerusalem at the Antonia Fortress. Their toughest task was keeping busy and fighting boredom. They regularly policed the streets and completed patrols to remind the populace that Rome was watching. Felix had taken ill over the past few weeks. He suffered from chills, vomiting, and a severe pain in his abdomen. He appeared to have caught Roman Fever, or modern-day malaria. It was called Roman Fever because of how it spread throughout the empire. Disease could take a legionnaire out of service as quickly as an enemy soldier. The Romans worked hard to combat disease even if they didn't understand it. For example, they learned that draining stagnant water was a good practice. Liborius was left in charge of the men, and Felix was sent to the medicus vulnerarius to recover.

After a few days, Liborius visited Felix at the Tenth Legion's infirmary to inquire about his recovery and then return. Felix was in a private room recovering; his eyes were open, but he did not look up when Liborius entered the room. His eyes were sunken, and he was drenched in sweat. Liborius paused for a moment beside the bed. He coughed softly. "Felix, the Tenth is missing a good centurion, and they have sent me to fetch you."

Felix stirred, looking up at Liborius. He wiped the perspiration from his forehead with his hand and drew a ragged breath. "I wish I could leap out of this bed and return to my men. I have had all manner of treatment; they had me on a bedbug diet and fed me the liver of a seven-year-old mouse. Tell me about my century."

Liborius filled Felix in with the boring details. Felix listened. He continued to wipe the sweat from his forehead.

"Liborius, I fear the Tenth will be stuck here for some time to back up Herod. But Herod with his vicious ways has it all wrong. There are certain truths in our existence that never change. You can reach all you want, but you will never touch a star. People may be ruled, but their hearts will never be conquered. Alexander the Great once said that whatever possession we gain by our sword cannot be sure or lasting, but the love gained by kindness and moderation is certain and durable. If Herod focused more on his people's hearts, he could win their loyalty, and the Tenth could move on to conquest instead of this waste of an assignment."

Liborius had never heard such emotion from Felix before. He let the words of Felix sink in. The conversation must have taken a lot out of Felix. His eyelids leaden, he looked ready to nod off. Liborius agreed with Felix and told him so. The meeting ended quickly. Felix fell asleep from exhaustion, and Liborius returned to his men.

The stars twinkled as Liborius looked up at the night sky out a window in the Antonia Fortress. A cool breeze gently touched his face. It was a particularly clear evening, and the stars were numerous. Liborius continued to watch the sky. He focused on the constellation

Orion. Orion is outlined by four bright stars at the corners of an imaginary trapezoid. Within the space defined by these four points, seeming to draw them together into a pattern, is a row of three stars tilted at an angle, called Orion's belt. Arcing downward from the belt is another group of fainter stars, his sword. *The sword*, Liborius thought to himself. *It will rust and damage if not maintained as a heart will falter if it's not shown kindness.* A shooting star appeared briefly and was gone. It was a beautiful sight but lasted only a blink as its twinkle ended. The clarity above became reflected in Liborius's mind, and before the sun set, he would set a plan in motion to learn the hearts of the Jews.

In Jerusalem, Herod made sure there was plenty of entertainment and funds for the legion. Any reasonable request for funds would be given. Instead of relying on an interpreter, Liborius convinced the legion to spend funds on teachers to educate a few soldiers in Hebrew. Liborius immersed himself in the study of Hebrew and was able to read a little and speak the language enough for simple conversation in a few weeks' time. Learning Hebrew was not an easy task. It used a different alphabet and had a right-to-left direction for reading and writing.

Liborius became fond of taking long walks in the city to listen to and practice the language. On one particular walk, he noticed a small crowd surrounding a man they addressed as "my master," which in Hebrew is *rabbi*. He learned from the crowd that the man's name was Shammai and that he was a teacher who traveled to interpret the Torah, explain the scriptures, and tell parables. The Torah for the Jews was the law of God as revealed to them by Moses, a major prophet who recorded the first five books of scripture. Some rabbis traveled from village to village, teaching in the synagogues. Though they relied on the hospitality of others, rabbis were never paid. They often took disciples who would study under their direction for years, traveling with them everywhere they went. Study sessions were often conducted outdoors in vineyards, marketplaces, beside a road, or in an open field. Liborius joined the crowd and listened to the speaker. The speaker was dressed in common clothing. He wore a tallit, a rectangle of heavy cloth that bore tassels on its four corners. This heavy cloth could be used as a blanket for sleeping. Underneath was the haluk, a linen tunic.

Shammai was telling this parable: "There are four types among those who sit in the presence of the rabbis: the sponge, the funnel, the strainer, and the sieve. The sponge, which soaks up everything. The funnel, which takes in at this end and lets out at the other. The strainer, which lets out the wine and retains the dregs. The sieve, which removes the chaff and retains the fine flour."[1]

The rabbi went on to explain the parable, that "the best disciple is not the sponge who retains absolutely everything, but the sieve who sifts through the teaching to retain what is best. We are to exercise wisdom and discernment, continually asking questions, weighing answers, seeding understanding within the context of God's word. Do not be a sponge, unquestioningly repeating whatever we learn from a favorite teacher."

The words and wisdom of the rabbi touched the heart of Liborius, and he desired to learn more about the Torah's teaching. Liborius would not enter a synagogue to learn, but he often made it a habit to listen in whenever a traveling rabbi spoke in Jerusalem.

Another notable rabbi he listened to was Hillel. Shammai was known for his strict approach to interpreting the laws of the Torah, but Hillel was known for his gentleness and moderate interpretation of the Law. His school of disciples often debated the disciples of Shammai over the stricter interpretations of Jewish Law. For example, they debated whether one should tell an ugly bride that she is beautiful. Shammai would say, "It is wrong to lie," and Hillel would argue, "All brides are beautiful on their wedding day." After one teaching, Hillel noticed Liborius who stood out to him. Liborius

---

1. *Pirkei Avot: Ethics of the Fathers* 5:15

was not in uniform but had the look of a soldier etched on his face and did not wear the local garb but the clothes of a Roman.

Hillel approached Liborius. "Greetings, my friend. I see you listened to me talk. Tell me what you found most interesting."

Liborius swallowed. "Your words about whatever I dislike, I should not do to my neighbor. That this principle sums up the whole Torah."

Hillel stared at him a moment longer and then nodded. "But do you know what that means?" he questioned. "I shall tell you. Do not do hateful acts to your neighbors. It is the Golden Rule of the Torah. Whatever you would that men should do to you, do you even to them."

Liborius thought for a moment and spoke, "Like an eye for an eye and a tooth for a tooth. If someone cuts off your arm, you cut off his arm."

Hillel chuckled slowly and finished with a glowing smile, "Not exactly. I have heard this quote before. It's from Hammurabi, the ancient King of Babylon. No, No. It's more like treating others like you would treat yourself."

Liborius thought for a moment. He closed his eyes briefly and then opened them. "I see. Thank you." He shook Hillel's hand, and Hillel returned the handshake warmly.

"I would not think to see a Roman here, though maybe not such a tall one," Hillel said.

Liborius's face reddened. "I am part of the Roman Empire, but I am originally from Gaul."

"I see. The Romans," Hillel spoke with authority. "I've heard they clear a city and call it peace."

Liborius replied, "I am a soldier of Rome. That is all I know. I don't always agree with the politicians, but I do what is asked of me."

Hillel frowned. "Many innocent people have died from a soldier just doing his duty. Following the Torah teaches a different kind of living. You live now as a soldier, but when you come home and the war is over, what then?"

Liborius placed his hands on his chin and thought. Emotions flooded him. This was never something he thought of before. "My dream was always to be a soldier, but now I am starting to see the dream of my former master, to settle one day and give up the soldier's life, to start a family." Liborius paused suddenly. His shoulders sagged, and there was anguish in his eyes. It was amazing how easy it was to talk to Hillel, but Liborius did not feel comfortable sharing everything. "I must return to my barracks now. Thank you, I enjoyed your teaching."

"What is your name?" Hillel spoke softly.

"Liborius." Liborius turned and began to walk away slowly.

"May God bless you," Hillel remarked at the back of Liborius.

CHAPTER XVII

PROMOTED

B ack in his barracks, Liborius learned that Felix had taken a turn for the worse and passed away. Liborius had a strong feeling that Felix would not make it, but he mourned, regardless. In an unexpected act, Liborius was quickly promoted to centurion by his commander to replace Felix. The body of Felix was cremated, and his ashes were placed in a vessel for transport to a permanent location at his family's burial site. The funeral did not cost Felix's family anything; a portion of each soldier's pay was set aside and pooled for funeral expenses from those in the Antonia garrison, including the ritual meal in which a portion of the sow used to sacrifice to Ceres for the departed was given to the living. In ancient Roman religion, Ceres was the goddess of agriculture, fertility, and motherly relationships.

The men under Liborius and the friends of Felix outside his sentry helped prepare the ritual meal to celebrate Felix's journey to the afterlife. They had tables placed outside the fortress filled with mostly local food—large amounts of bread, cooked grains, and roasted legumes. Olive oil from the many olive trees of the hill country was available. And not to be missed, there was watered-down wine, the favorite drink of a legionnaire, in abundance. Liborius ate and drank heartily with his men. The meal started at noon, and it was now approaching sunset. The overeating and drinking made Liborius very lethargic, and he could barely see through his shuttering eyelids. He was starting to doze lightly when he was startled by a man hollering.

"Centurion!" yelled the man angrily. The man of medium height wore the costly garb of a Jewish aristocrat. Liborius was not happy to be awaken, and he did his best to stand up with dignity.

"I am in command. What is it?" Liborius challenged the man.

The Jew said, "Your men have raided my stores and taken my wine. The damage is considerable." The man scowled. "I demand justice and compensation for what they have done."

Liborius absorbed the news and then spoke irritably. "This is a strong accusation. What proof do you have?"

The Jew's mouth tightened in anger, and he flashed rage, suppressed as soon as it began. "My men tried to stop them, but they were too late. They left this among the broken jars."

The Jew handed Liborius a gladius. With a quick examination of the blade, Liborius found a name inscribed on it and the mark of the Tenth Legion. "I will investigate this at once," Liborius reluctantly told the man. Your name, please, and directions to your winery so I may give you the results of my inquiry."

The man was not pleased, but a look into the eyes of Liborus and he knew Liborius was serious. "I am called Daniel from the tribe of Levi." Daniel gave directions to his winery and departed.

A few men at the feast started to approach the newly promoted centurion to talk. "I will deal with this in the morning," Liborius said, waving them off and expeditiously making it to his bed to sleep off the wine.

In the early morning, with the sun still resolutely below the horizon, Liborius quickly began his investigation. The hills of Judea near Jerusalem had been covered with grape vines at least since the days of King David and King Solomon. It was common to carve presses and have fermentation vats out of solid rock. The cool summer nights and limestone-rich soil produced very fine wine from grapes. The vineyards in Judea were a major export and economic mainstay for King Herod. Wine could be used for drinking, medical purposes, cleaning homes, and dyeing cloth. It was so valuable that it could be used as currency for paying tribute. Liborius was furious with his men as disrupting the flow of wine was a serious offense, especially for a disciplined soldier of Rome. In short order, he had the proof he needed. The answers were literally beaten out of the men. With Felix gone, Liborius was in charge and passed judgment swiftly. He had the five perpetrators whipped in full view of the entire legion. Then he warned his men to behave and gave strict orders not to bother the vineyards, especially Daniel's. He considered the matter closed. For his last act, he used his own funds to send money to Daniel for the damages caused by his men.

A week after judgment, Liborius was sleeping when he was awakened by Ailean shaking him. Ailean was one of the slaves assigned to serve the contubernium that the wine offenders were part of. Ailean was not much bigger than the average 18-year-old, but there was no doubting his years. He had a biracial look, lighter skinned but with African features, with a hooked nose and dark eyes.

With a panic-stricken look on his face, Ailean stuttered, "I have some news, I must tell you, but first I beg to be under your protection."

Liborius did not hesitate. "You have it. Now what is it?"

"The men in my contubernium I serve have just departed. They intend to poison the well at the vineyard to retaliate against the man who complained."

Liborius's face reddened. "Go to my quarters, and do not leave until I return." Liborius quickly dressed and assembled a force of 30 men he could round up on short notice and then raced to the vineyard. Not all the men had time to be dressed in armor, but every man had his gladius. Heart pounding, Liborius pushed his men hard in a run. Echoes of thunder rolled across the night sky, and rain fell. The rain, slow to start, splattered the ground randomly. Then it fell like buckets. The rain kept pouring, adding weight to their soaked clothes, but the men pushed on.

The rain stopped as they arrived at the vineyard. The clouds slowly departed, and sunlight escaped the air as dawn arrived. Liborius did not allow a moment for the men to catch their breath. He ordered his men to spread out across the vineyard. Amazingly, they caught the men in the act of pouring poison into the well. Liborius, with a sword in his hand, ordered the miscreants to surrender. He tightened his grip on his sword and peered at the miscreants with hatred in his eyes. It was difficult for him not to give the order to slay the men on the spot. He glowered at them but kept his mouth shut. The villains froze in fear with no options available, surrendering without a struggle. They were quickly arrested and sent back to be dealt with. Disobeying direct orders, the only outcome would be death. The Roman Army did not play games.

Liborius knocked on Daniel's door. Daniel was awake when he heard the commotion but was too scared to go outside. Daniel opened the door cautiously and invited Liborius inside. With a cold knot in the pit of his belly, Liborius explained what had happened and promised to send money to build another well. To further make amends, he offered his own money to build a new synagogue. He was disappointed in his men and did not want to have any trouble with the Jews or King Herod. He had begun to develop a fondness for the Jewish people. He could not even think about what happened without his stomach twisting.

Daniel listened to Liborius silently and then spoke glumly. "I thank you for what you have done to protect my vineyard. You are generous, but why use your own money to build a synagogue?"

Liborius thought for a moment. "It's the principle of the thing, and these were my men."

Daniel sighed. "I am not happy with what has happened, but I feel justice has been done."

Liborius returned to the barracks inside the Antonia Fortress and immediately went to see Ailean. The slave had patiently waited for Liborius to return and became quite anxious hearing what happened.

"Ailean, I wish to thank you for coming to me with the information on your contubernium. It was the right decision to make. You are a slave of the Roman Army. I offer you the opportunity to be my attendant. I will treat you fairly and pay you for your labor. In time, you can earn your freedom."

Ailean grinned with the favorable circumstances and answered Liborius confidently. "Tha . . . Thank you, centurion. I will not let you down."

"I know you will not, Ailean. You have proved to be a man of integrity, and I am honored to have you assist me. Please call me Liborius." Having slept very little, Liborius was exhausted and yawned. "I will see you in the morning."

The next day, Ailean began performing the tasks Liborius used to complete for Lucius. Liborius fulfilled his promise to Ailean, treating him fairly and giving him payment. Ailean was loyal to Liborius, going above and beyond his duty whenever he could. A strong bond formed between Liborius and Ailean with each respecting the other. Ailean and Liborius shared similar interests and both especially enjoyed taking long walks together through Jerusalem in conversation, always stopping to hear the traveling rabbis deliver eulogies. Ailean eventually saved enough money from a generous Liborius and paid for his freedom from the Roman Army. He stayed with Liborius as his servant and friend. They continued to travel together and enjoy the sermons by the rabbis. Together, they began to pray to the God of Israel in private. When they were in public, they would pray in their hearts and minds. Jews prayed fixed prayers at fixed times, but they subscribed to a rabbi who warned them they should pray spontaneously at any time. He also told them to be wise in prayer, giving them an example that if they heard a cry of distress, they should refrain from praying that the cry did not come from their friends. It would not be reasonable to ask God to wish evil on others for the sake of the people they love.

The synagogue that Liborius funded was finally built in Capernaum, and Liborius was there for the morning dedication. As expected for such a sacred building, it was found at the highest point in town. Money had been lavished on this beautiful synagogue. It was built almost entirely of imported, white calcareous stones rather than the smaller stones of black basalt used for most of the town's construction. Liborius sold Lucius's former home in Rome to fund the project, but he was glad to do it. The Jews thanked him and called him a friend. There were not many Romans who earned the title of friend with the Jewish people, and this title was worth more to him than all the money he spent.

After the dedication, Liborius gave himself up to his own thoughts, first to musing about the Jews and then to wondering about retirement. He felt comfortable in Israel and had a sense of peace there. Maybe he would move to beautiful Caesarea on the coast. This site of the former Phoenician naval station had been awarded to King Herod. At first, Herod built a grand palace there jutting out into the sea and then went on to build a large port and city, which he named in honor of his patron Caesar Augustus, formerly Octavian. Roman aqueducts brought in water, and a huge theater was built. With plenty of money remaining from his inheritance, Liborius had many options. He continued his duties as a centurion but began to dream as his former master, Lucius, had of life after the military.

CHAPTER XVIII

A JOURNEY

Herod sat, tapping his fingers methodically on his ornate, carved, golden chair. He was dressed in an elegant cloak, and his hair was specially trimmed to look like a Roman caesar. His so-called advisor stood in front of him, shaking with nervousness. No one could really advise Herod.

Herod looked him straight in the eye, not blinking, and said, "I asked for your report, did I not?" The man appeared to reply, but before he could speak, Herod snapped, "Guards! Take him away and have him executed at once for treason. He obviously is not loyal to his king!" The advisor wet himself as the guards roughly dragged him away for execution.

As time went on, Herod the Great, or Herod the Wicked, as he was called by the Jews behind his back, became extremely paranoid about losing the throne. The paranoia also included his family. Suspecting his wife, Mariamme, of being unfaithful, he had her executed. The two sons he fathered with her were suspected of disloyalty and executed as well. The family avoided Herod as much as possible, feeling safer to avoid the angry, violent ruler. This isolation may have driven Herod further into his madness.

When wise men, who had seen a star in the east, revealed that the new "King of the Jews" had been born and they therefore wanted to pay him homage, Herod became very fearful. He assembled the chief priests and scribes of the people and asked them where the "Anointed One," the Messiah, was to be born. "But you, Bethlehem, in the land of Judah, are by no means least among the rulers of Judah; for out of you will come a ruler who will be the shepherd of my people Israel."[1] After hearing this, Herod sent the magi to Bethlehem, instructing them to search for the child and, after they found him, to report to him so he may go and worship him. However, after they found the child Jesus, they were warned in a dream not to report back to Herod. Similarly, Joseph, the child's father, was warned in a dream that Herod intended to kill Jesus, so he and his family fled to Egypt. When Herod realized he had been made a fool, he gave orders to slaughter all boys ages two and younger in Bethlehem and the surrounding area.

Herod's madness continued, and he even killed his eldest son, Antipater, two years later, only five days before his own death. The paranoid king, suffering severe health problems that affected his internal organs, finally died, and his kingdom was divided among three of his remaining sons and his sister. Octavian, known as Augustus, had the last say and intervened, not giving the title of king to any of them. He did not want another Herod. They were made puppet rulers, and Judea, Samaria, and Idumea became a proper Roman province called Iudea, ruled by a Roman governor.

Coponius was the first governor of the Iudean province. He, like most Roman governors, had the power of life and death over his subjects. Jewish opposition started early under the Roman yoke, and during his governorship, the revolt of Judas the Galilean took place.

---

1. Matt. 2:6

Coponius was recalled to Rome and replaced by Marcus Ambivulus. Marcus, originally a cavalry officer, ruled until he was succeeded by Annius Rufus. Annius was succeeded by Valerius Gratus. Gratus was disliked by his subjects for the frequent changes in the appointment of the high priest. He was replaced by the infamous Pontius Pilate.

As governor of Judea, Pilate repeatedly caused near rebellion among the Jews because of his insensitivity to Jewish customs. While Pilate's predecessors had respected Jewish customs by removing all images and effigies on their standards when entering Jerusalem, Pilate allowed his soldiers to bring them into the city at night. When the citizens of Jerusalem discovered them the following day, they appealed to Pilate to remove the ensigns of Caesar from the city. After five days of deliberation, Pilate had his soldiers surround the demonstrators and threaten them with death, which they were willing to accept rather than submit to desecration of the Mosaic Law. Pilate finally removed the images just before a massacre happened.

Pilate even upset the reigning Roman Emperor Tiberius after antagonizing the Jews by setting up gold-coated shields in Herod's palace in Jerusalem. The shields were supposed to honor Tiberius, but the shields were set up simply to annoy the Jews. The Jews protested the installation of the shields, first to Pilate and then, when he declined to remove them, by writing to Tiberius. It is reported that upon reading the letters, Tiberius wrote to Pilate with a host of reproaches for his audacious violation of precedent and bade him at once to take down the shields and have them transferred from the capital to Caesarea. In another incident, Pilate spent money from the Temple to build an aqueduct. Pilate had soldiers hidden in the crowd of Jews while addressing them, and when Jews again protested his actions, he gave the signal for his soldiers to attack, beat, and kill the Jewish petitioners in an attempt to silence them. Pilate was vindictive and had a furious temper. His habit of insulting Jews, along with his cruelty and continued murders of the untried and uncondemned, made life painful for the Jews.

Besides Pilate, the Jews suffered under Roman occupation. Not only did Rome demand oppressively high taxes, it also harshly repressed every hint of opposition. In Sepphoris, a town three miles from Nazareth, the Romans quelled a rebellion by burning the city to the ground and then selling its survivors into slavery. The Jewish people cried out to God daily, begging for Messiah to deliver them.

Liborius decided to build his house in Capernaum, not too far from the synagogue he built. He decided against the lavish city of Caesarea. Capernaum was a fishing village located on the northern shore of the Sea of Galilee and located not far from Bethsaida. Capernaum had a small population of about 1,500. Liborius's home was typical of the area. He used the local black basalt stones. He reinforced the basalt with crushed stones and mud without using mortar. The most lavish part of the house was the open courtyard where there was a circular furnace made of heat-resistant earth, as well as grain mills and a set of stone stairs that led to the roof. The entire floor of the house was cobbled. Around the courtyard, modest rooms were arranged to receive a kiss of sunlight through a series of openings. The home was large enough to have a kitchen and bread oven. A small stable was built adjacent to the courtyard. Ailean moved in immediately and kept the home up for Liborius. Liborius commuted to Jerusalem to be with the legion and was not home that often. Although his visits were short, he was able to make many friends in Capernaum.

In Jerusalem, Liborius's commander gave him a task to deliver a letter from a Roman publican. Publicans served as public contractors; in addition, they served as tax collectors for Rome, bidding on contracts for the collection of various types of taxes. The letter was to be delivered to Matthew, the tax collector in Capernaum. Liborius was selected because the commander knew Liborius had a home there and would be able to locate Matthew quickly. Liborius appreciated the assignment and looked forward to visiting his home. Choosing not to take any men with him, he decided to travel alone.

The uniform of a soldier and a gladius were his only companions. He wore the lorica segmentata that consisted of metal strips fastened to internal leather straps with shoulder guards. Breastplates and backplates added further protection.

He set out on the northern road that led out from the city. The small road was nothing like the construction of the Roman roads. These roads were mostly dirt with some stone from time to time. The Hebrew word for road means a beaten, worn-out path. This road truly was. He traveled over the hills of Judea, passing by the site of Bethel and descending into a small plain before rising again to the hills of Samaria under the shadow of Mount Gerizim and Mount Ebal. Through Samaria, he passed the foot of Mount Gilboa across the Plain of Esdraelon and took the fork toward Capernaum.

Exhausted and dusty from travel, Liborius decided to take a short rest in Genneseret just a few miles outside his destination. Genneseret was a town blessed with rich earth. It was said the fruits of Gennesaret had such respect among the rabbis that they were not allowed in Jerusalem at the time of the feasts because the people might be tempted to come merely for their indulgence. The Jewish tradition recommended keeping an open house for the benefit of strangers, but Liborius searched out a public inn to stay for the night. He did not want to inconvenience anyone with a visit from a Roman centurion. It was late afternoon when he arrived at the first inn he found. He was met by an innkeeper who was more than stout, with a plump face and a very long beard. After payment was arranged, the innkeeper brought Liborius to a small room with bedding rolled out on the floor. The innkeeper handed Liborius a small oil lamp for lighting if it was needed and then departed. Bit by bit, he forced his muscles to let him straighten his legs and lie flat on the bedding. Outside, the falling rain began. It fell with a soft tap, tap, tap sound that soothed him. The comforting sound made him feel drowsy, and he fell asleep.

Liborius stifled a yawn mid-morning when he awoke from his exhausted sleep. He decided to visit the local market just outside the town walls to look around. It was a beautiful day with fluffy, white clouds that drifted in a soft, blue sky, and the breeze was just right. Taking off his helmet, his brown curls clung to his head in a sweat-curled mat. He watched as people purchased their goods and then lingered to talk and socialize. He watched the children as they ran and played games in the market. Children whose lives were hard and routine always loved to go to the market where so many interesting things were happening. Liborius purchased and feasted on walnuts, olives, and figs. He was just about to finish eating when a small boy suddenly crashed into him, sending his remaining figs flying to the ground. The young boy, about 10 years old, looked up and quickly studied the man he had run into. The boy's face took fright, and he immediately began apologizing and begging for forgiveness. With a smile, Liborius cut him off. "It's quite fine. No harm done here." He blew the dust off a fig and handed one to the boy. The boy ate it cautiously. Then Liborius picked up the figs that had fallen and finished them off with the boy. The boy relaxed, and they talked for a while.

The boy's name was Nathan, a brown-haired boy with windswept locks matted and dull. He was skinny, and his clothes hung on him. The boy, in fact, was 12 years old, being raised by his mother, a widow. A widow, Liborius knew, would scarcely provide food for the boy and had little to offer him besides her love. With minimal, if any, inheritance rights, she was likely in no-man's land. A widow had already left her own family, and with her husband's death, the bond between her and his family was fragile. The boy had no memory of his father.

They had a few laughs as Liborius told the boy all the child-appropriate jokes he could remember. "A sage came to check in on a friend who was gravely ill. When the man's wife said that he had departed, the intellectual replied, 'When he arrives back, will you tell him that I stopped by?'"

Nathan giggled and told one of his own. "One man complains to another slave, 'The slave you sold me died!' 'By the gods!' the other replied. 'During the time he was in my service, he never did such a thing.'" Liborius burst out laughing like thunder in a low, rumbling boom.

It did not take long for the boy's mother to find her child. The look on her face told Liborius that she was the boy's mother. The poor clothes on the woman did not hide that she was a beautiful woman. Her hair was straight black, her eyes dark, and her figure a perfect hourglass. The mother tried to hide her emotions on her innocent face. Her anguish was evident in the crease of her lovely brow and the down curve of her full lips. But those eyes; her eyes showed her heart. She immediately scolded the boy for troubling Liborius. Then she looked up at Liborius, her dark brown eyes hunting for some hint of what Liborius intended. Liborius was at a loss for words and simply stood admiring her. His heart had never pounded before with such emotion. He was falling for her by the second. He flushed furiously and tried to focus. Before Liborius could utter a word, she proceeded to drag the boy from the market.

"Wait, please," he laughed. "The boy has done me no harm."

The woman stopped and turned to look at Liborius. She was surprised to hear Hebrew from a Roman soldier and stuttered. "My apologies. The boy will not bother you anymore."

Liborius shuffled his feet. "As I told you, the boy has done no harm. We were simply sharing some figs. Nathan is a good boy. You should be proud." Liborius smiled softly.

"We are late. We must be going. Come on, Nathan." She grabbed the boy's arm and off they went.

"God bless you," Liborius spoke to her back.

Abigail's steps slowed. She turned to Liborius. "You are a strange Roman, are you not?"

Liborius smiled, "I am who I am. Tell me, what is your name?"

"My name is Abigail."

Liborius knew the meaning of the name in Hebrew. "You truly must be your father's joy." Liborius bumbled awkwardly.

Abigail did not crack a smile, but Liborius heard it in her voice. "And are you your father's joy?"

Liborius thought for a moment and put his head down slightly. "I never really knew my father, but the man I served would be like a father. I would like to think he would be proud of me. I am headed to my home nearby in Capernaum on an errand. My home is never a stumbling block to those in need."

Her eyes were a bottomless pool of darkness with a bundle of sorrow swimming in them, and he wanted to, no, needed to offer something to help her. But he saw strength and pride in her eyes, and he knew she would never accept his help.

"Thank you for being friendly to my son, though he may be taught not to do that again." She looked at the boy who frowned, and then turned to Liborius. "I see in your eyes your friendship is genuine. You are a good fruit." Liborius looked confused. Abigail smiled. "I recently heard a rabbi teaching from a boat by the lake of Gennesaret because the crowds were pressing in on him to hear the word of God. He said, "No good tree bears bad fruit, nor does a bad tree bear good fruit. Each tree is recognized by its own fruit. People do not pick figs from thornbushes, or grapes from briers"[2]

Liborius nodded. "This rabbi sounds interesting. What is his name?"

Abigail's dark eyes shined with joy. "His name is Jesus of Nazareth. May God bless you and see you safely on your journey. We must be on our way."

Liborius watched as Abigail and Nathan walked away. He would have loved to follow and talk more to Abigail. He couldn't get her out of his head. She was so beautiful, and her name to him was a work of art. He imagined running after her but feared his uniform would cause a stir. He laughed to himself. Not much romance in the life of a centurion. He left the market and continued his travels to Capernaum.

---

2. Luke 6:43–44

CHAPTER XIX

TIME FOR CHANGE

The sunshine was warm in its brilliance as Liborius continued his walk to Capernaum. The heavily worn road was clearly marked. Surrounding the road was a wide area with little vegetation. His throat became parched, and he drew a big gulp from a leather bag he carried with him. While wiping his mouth with his hand, he noticed a small thicket of growth with a large fig tree nearly 20 feet in height and with large leaves that would provide pleasant shade. *What a great place to rest*, thought Liborius. He imagined a short nap under the tree. He took a few steps toward the tree. A man stepped out from the tree, a sling whirling round his head. Something struck Liborius's helmet, and darkness took everything.

Liborius awoke to the smell of tallow candles that lit a large tent. Even with the candlelight, the inside of the tent was rather dark. He struggled to raise himself to a sitting position. He hurt from the blow to his head. The ties on his wrists and ankles were bound tightly, biting into his flesh.

"So you are awake," came a rough voice.

"That I am." Liborius turned to the miscreant with angry eyes. The man wore local clothing, a simple, well-worn, gray woolen tunic. He had black hair and a dark beard with a few flecks of gray in it. He radiated danger the way a fire gave heat. At a quick glance, Liborius noticed two other men in the tent and his sword leaning against his helmet a good distance away.

"What is the meaning of this?" Liborius glowered.

The man speaking to Liborius looked startled for an instant, hearing the words of Hebrew from a Roman soldier, but it did not last long.

"You want something, or you would have killed me," spoke a defiant Liborius.

"Yes, we can kill you and bury your body in a hole, and none would ever know. We usually do our mischief at night until we have enough. But seeing you are a centurion—if I'm not mistaken, your rank from the headdress on your helmet would mean you surely have some gold on you—but you have very little on you, just a letter addressed to Matthew. So, what to do with you?"

The face of Liborius flushed with anger. He wished desperately he could grab his sword from across the tent. "You can let me go!" Liborius cried in anger. "But if gold is what you want, I can do plenty. Capernaum is not far from here. I have a home there. My servant Ailean will pay you my ransom."

The man thought and then gave a wicked grin. "After the ransom, you will surely go after us."

Liborius swallowed and struggled to keep his voice level. "I also give you my word that I will not seek you out to hang you upon the cross. I swear! On my honor as a centurion and a vow to the God of Israel."

"You, a Roman soldier, vow to the God of Israel?" The man scoffed. "Do you play me for a fool?"

Liborius quickly quoted a few lines from the Torah and spoke. "I am still a student, but I know God's wrath is to be feared."

The man nodded. "These are tough times. I will take your offer," he smirked. "Fifty gold pieces, if you please, to this humble robber. Now write a letter that we may take to your servant and be done with this."

The ties on Liborius's wrist were cut, and he immediately wrote the letter that was quickly dispatched to Capernaum. The gold did not take long to be delivered. The sun was just barely risen when Liborius was awakened with a not-so-gentle kick to his side. Liborius was blindfolded and led back to the road. The binds on Liborius were cut.

"Go, centurion, and honor your word. You will remember me so you may have a name for your image. I am Dysmas. Do not take it personal, centurion, it was only business. Someday I will pay for my sins, but today is not that day."

Liborus grumbled, "Only business to rob from your own people?"

"Your sword, centurion."

Liborius watched his sword as it was tossed in front of his feet. He froze for a second when he grabbed it, but he had given his word. He sheathed his sword hard. "Do not judge what you do not know about a centurion. These are tough times. We do what we need to do for survival. Goodbye."

"May the rest of your journey be safe," Dysmas answered with a crooked smile.

The band of robbers quickly departed, leaving Liborius alone on the road. Liborius stretched his muscles and rubbed his arms. His body ached from being bound. His stomach growled, and his throat was parched. His captors did not feed him or give him drink. His water bag was not returned to him. He felt drained and empty but pushed himself to move on down the road. Black clouds draped across the sky, rising from the east. Thunder rolled across the sky. Then there was the sprinkling of tiny raindrops. Liborius cursed his luck as it began to pour, soaking his clothing as well as his spirits. Lightning flashed above him. He found a rocky enclave to shelter and wait until the rain subsided and the storm passed. Alone with his thoughts, he prayed for strength and for the storm to end. He longed to get to Capernaum, deliver the letter to Matthew, and then spend time at home. When the storm passed, he drank a few sips of water from a muddy puddle and then set out as fast as his feet could carry him.

A tired and miserable Liborius finally entered Capernaum. An important crossroad for collecting custom taxes for Rome, Capernaum was on the grand Via Maris highway that connected the Roman Empire along the Mediterranean Sea. Liborius was filthy, and his foul odor told him that he needed a bath badly. He did not care. He wanted to accomplish his mission first. Wasting no time, he immediately went to the house of Matthew, the tax collector. The home was similar in construction to other houses in Capernaum, made with dry, coarse, black basalt stone walls with a roof made of crisscrossed tree branches cemented by a mixture of straw and earth. Liborius knocked on the door and was led in by Matthew. Matthew was of average height with deep brown eyes to match his rich brown hair. He had a short, dark beard. His large, flowing beige and black striped outer tunic was of good quality and tied with a belt decorated with embroidery. There was an air about Matthew that if he spoke, people listened. Liborius, not wanting to delay, took out the crumpled letter as he followed Matthew.

Matthew invited him into a large plastered room and took the letter. Matthew read the letter, his face turning to disgust. "They want more money. They hate me enough. No one likes to pay money to any government, especially when the government is an oppressive regime." Matthew caught himself looking at Liborius's uniform. Liborius did not appear to mind. The local tax collectors were Jews who worked for the hated Romans. These individuals were seen as turncoats, traitors to their own countrymen, enriching themselves at the expense of their fellow Jews. It was common knowledge that most tax collectors cheated the people they collected from. They often collected more than required and kept the extra for themselves.

Everyone just understood that was how it worked. With a sigh, Matthew wrote a quick note that he would accept the charge and handed it to Liborius to send back to the Roman publican with his return trip to Jerusalem.

"Some wine before you leave?" offered Matthew. "If I may, you look like you could use some."

Liborius gave a short, uneasy nod. His thirst was great, and he gulped a little too quickly as wine spilled from his mouth and chin. He wiped his face with his hand.

Matthew spoke. "Thank you for bringing this letter to me. I now have a good amount of work to do. If you would excuse me, I'm sure you have a better place to be than spending time in a tax collector's home."

Task complete, Liborius departed quickly and went home. At home, Liborius found a rich aroma of food greeting him from inside. *What perfect timing*, he thought to himself. He opened the door and found Ailean cooking the evening meal in the courtyard. The smell of roasted lamb made Liborius salivate in anticipation. Ailean's eyes fell upon Liborius. "I prayed you would be home today!" Ailean embraced his friend in a great hug. Ailean laughed, "You stink something fierce, but I'm sure you would like to eat before you bathe. I have the table set already. Please have a seat, and I will bring over the lamb."

Liborius went to the small table set for two and took a seat. The smell of warm bread with a slab of melted yellow butter beckoned to him. Next to it was a wooden bowl of mixed vegetables with beans and lentils. Liborius's stomach growled as he waited patiently for Ailean to join him. He grabbed a few olives from the table and stuffed them in his mouth. *It is great to be back home and have a real meal*, he thought to himself. *This is where my heart is.*

Ailean was not long. He brought over the roast lamb and set a thick, hearty slice on Liborius's plate. Ailean served himself a slice and then said a quick blessing for the food. The men dug in. Liborius felt no need for pretentious manners and grabbed the lamb, ripping a chunk off with his teeth.

"So what news since I've been away?" Liborius barely got it out with his mouth still stuffed with food. He then gulped a full cup of wine.

Ailean's face lit up. "Very interesting news, indeed. The talk of Capernaum is about a rabbi named Jesus. While you were away, Jesus from Nazareth—not that far from here, about 20 miles—performed a miraculous healing at a synagogue." The eyes of Ailean swelled with admiration. "It was on the Sabbath, which really angered the priests there. Jesus told the man with a shriveled hand, 'Get up and stand here.' Then Jesus said to them, 'I will ask you one thing. Is it lawful on the Sabbath to do good or to do evil, to save life or to destroy?'[1] And when he had looked around at them all, he told the man to stretch out his hand. He did, and his hand was restored. They were filled with rage and, I bet, discussing what they might do to Jesus. Can you believe the anger over healing a man? If God lived on earth, people would surely break his windows."

Liborius agreed with Ailean that it made no sense. Liborius scratched his head. "I'm the least of an expert on the Torah than nearly any man of Israel, but I believe Jesus was correct to heal the man. I would love to hear Jesus preach and learn more about this rabbi. I will stay a while in Capernaum long enough to hear Jesus speak, if I can."

Ailean turned toward Liborius with a mischievous grin. "Great to have you back for a while. Who else can I beat at Hounds and Jackals?"

Dark eyes large with shock, Liborius gave a raucous snort of laughter. "Ailean, you beat everyone."

"I know, but you put up the best fight," Ailean spoke sarcastically.

---

1. See Luke 9.

Liborius put on the best icy stare he could. "This time, I'm going to defeat you." They both laughed.

Liborius and Ailean finished the meal and then played the board game Hounds and Jackals. Originally an Egyptian game, it was played all over Israel and around the Mediterranean. They moved their peg pieces, representing either a hound or a jackal, along the board with holes cut in it. Both players threw sticks instead of dice. First, the players tossed their sticks to determine who went first. Whoever scored the lowest went first moving the exact number of holes they scored with their stick. Then, the opponent threw the sticks again and moved the number of holes they scored. They played several games that Ailean won easily. Liborius and Ailean had quite a few cups of wine to celebrate the return of Liborius. It was late when Liborius staggered toward his bed. Tiredness swallowed him whole.

In a dream, Liborius was standing in a field of green wheat, the stalks bent lazily in the wind. He ran his hand along them to feel the combination of rough and smooth and then held his face upward to feel the warm light of the summer day. He started walking. He could see puffs of gray smoke in the distance and followed. The smoke led him to a village. He could hear screams as he approached. The village was being sacked by the Roman Army. The people were massacred. He needed to learn why. He ran into the village. He spotted a group of Roman soldiers entering a home. He followed. The soldiers pulled out their swords and approached the inhabitants, a woman and a young boy. They were dressed poorly and looked half starved. Liborius hollered, "Stop immediately!" The men ignored him. They came closer to the woman and child. Liborius grabbed for the men, but his arm passed through them. The men proceeded to butcher the woman and young boy in front of him. He hollered and tried to get their attention, but it was no use. The soldiers ransacked the home looking for valuables and then ran out of the home. Liborius stood looking at the bloody bodies. The faces were familiar. They were Abigail and Nathan. He screamed.

Liborius woke as his heart pounded in the blackness of the room. In the blackness, he moved slowly to sit up in bed. He trembled a little. Even though it was a dream, he wished he could do something. He punched the bed. *They were following orders*, he thought to himself. *Many innocent people have died from a soldier just doing his duty.* The words of Hillel the rabbi burst into his mind. It was not the first time he had thought of going to his commander to ask for retirement. Liborius still had plenty of wealth from his inheritance. The Legion was not at war. The commander would not deny his request. *Soon*, he thought, *soon.*

CHAPTER XX
STAYING FOR GOOD

Getting out of bed, Liborius put on his comfortable woolen tunic dyed a walnut color. He then paused, looking at his sword that was still leaning against his bedroom wall and his uniform tossed in a neat pile on the floor. His dirty uniform was in desperate need of cleaning and mending from his walk to Capernaum. He put on a thin outer robe of earthen color. The only detail that marked him as a Roman soldier were the well-worn, hobnailed military sandals he put on. A risen sun poured heat and light into the room as he made his way out. The rumpled bed blankets were the only proof that anyone had stayed there. He never stayed long enough in Capernaum to put down roots or make it any kind of a home. *Well, I'm staying for good soon*, he believed. Turning his back on the already unoccupied room, he went out.

Ailean met Liborius in the courtyard and said, "I was thinking maybe for your return trip to Jerusalem, you should ride. The trip would be quicker, and I wouldn't have so much work to do on your uniform."

Liborius grinned. "You know, Ailean, that's not a bad idea. At least I can finally have an animal in the stable." He motioned to the stable adjacent to his courtyard. "My journey here was not exactly luxurious. I would love to be more comfortable on my return trip. Go and purchase a donkey for my travel back. I don't want a horse. I have no time to learn to ride, nor do I want to spend the money."

Ailean looked at him thoughtfully. "It is better to ride a donkey that carries you than a horse that throws you. I will fetch a worthy one and also try to find where Jesus will be teaching." Ailean departed.

Liborius grew tired waiting for Ailean and decided to work and pull weeds in their garden just outside the home. Ailean had kept the garden well, and there was little to do. They grew beans, lentils, cucumbers, and onions. He took his robe off and folded it neatly on the ground. With the warm sun shining brightly, he began to sweat as he pulled weeds by hand. Working the earth and getting his fingers dirty felt deeply relaxing. *Dirt is easier to wash off than blood,* Liborius thought. He continued to toil in the haze of the afternoon. He could feel his loose shirt start to cling to his back in places and a slight sting to his eyes. He stood back, satisfied with his work.

A loud, braying noise that went on for several seconds startled him. He stretched his back after all his bending, and Ailean appeared with the donkey. "No word about where Jesus will teach next. I'm sure we will hear something soon. I acquired a good donkey already trained for riding." Ailean petted the tuft of hair on the donkey's head. "She has a bridle bit made of copper. Don't worry. I got her for a fair price. She is rather gentle. Now, what to name her."

Liborius studied the dark, gray donkey for a moment. Passing his fingers through his own gray, he remembered the attractive but stubborn woman he met in Genneseret. "Let's call her Abigail." Ailean nodded and then departed to the stable. Liborius paused to admire his garden work and went inside to dry off and refresh.

A week went by, and there was no word about the rabbi named Jesus. Capernaum, a large, Galilean fishing village and busy trading center, was not heavily populated. The population was about 1,500. If Jesus was teaching, it would not take long for word to get around. Liborius made himself comfortable at home and visited friends, both Jews and Romans. He often visited the basalt synagogue he had constructed, hoping to find Jesus teaching there. Jesus was known to teach in this local synagogue but had not visited recently. Liborius continued taking long walks with Ailean in Capernaum. It seemed like ages since they had walked together in Jerusalem. They were on a walk now toward the northwest shore of the Sea of Galilee to see the water and watch the busy fishing boats come in. Caravans stopped at Capernaum to resupply themselves with produce and dried fish. The fishermen made a decent enough living to support themselves in Capernaum.

Ailean walked unusually slow today as if his brain were struggling to tell each foot to take the next step. Liborius slowed his pace to match the steps of Ailean, and his mind focused on the gentle footsteps that seemed to echo on the empty dirt road. Ailean suddenly stumbled, and with each step, his stomach tightened and ached as he began to sweat and feel nauseous. He tried to swallow as his throat clenched, but no matter what, he could not stop the warmth rising from his chest. Ailean buckled over and vomited.

"You feel better my friend to get that out?" Liborius spoke in a nervous tone.

"A little, but I don't feel like finishing the walk."

"Let's go home; I walked enough today." Liborius slapped Ailean on the back softly. Ailean wiped his face clean, and determination set in on his face to hide his emotions. Both men hurried home.

The next morning, Ailean did not rise from bed before Liborius, as usual. Liborius decided to get the morning water and leave Ailean undisturbed. He remembered that Ailean did look the worse for the wear yesterday. An adequate water source was located at the western edge of the village, but Liborius decided to go to the main city well. He took a large, earthen pitcher and headed out in the cool morning.

He was not the first to get to the well that morning, and a short line awaited him. A large group of women surrounded the well. This was the time of day when they talked with their friends, waiting to draw water. Most of the women in the village recognized Liborius and nodded or smiled politely at him.

"Where is your servant Ailean today?" an older woman asked. "This is the first time we have seen you fetch water." She was not overly old, but her body had matured past her years so much that she wore the wizened features of an old crone.

"Oh, he decided to sleep in today," Liborius spoke jokingly. "I can use the morning exercise."

"Well, don't turn this into a habit. We enjoy Ailean's humor every morning and his skill at riddles. The last one he told goes like this. 'Like a fish in a fish pond, like troops before the king.' I still can't figure it out."

Liborius had heard this one before. "The next time you see Ailean, you tell him a broken bow is the answer. You see, a broken bow is as useless as a fish not caught but still swims in the well, or as troops who do not fight in battle but remain in front of the king." She winked at him, and Liborius laughed out loud.

Liborius returned home where Ailean was still asleep and decided to make breakfast. Typically, it was skipped, but Liborius wanted to feel useful. Making his way to the kitchen, he found what he needed in the small niches cut into the walls. He mixed barley grain with water, kneaded in fermented dough, and left it to rise for about an hour. Then the thin, flat circles of dough were slapped into the bread oven. The aroma of the cooking bread called to Ailean as he made his way into the kitchen. Ailean staggered in bleary-eyed, looking like a lion had run over him.

"Good morning, Liborius. I thought I smelled something burning."

Liborius stared at him in mock anger. "Good to see someone using that oven. I prefer to cook the bread on hot stones over fire in the courtyard."

Ailean's head lowered. "I overslept. I wanted to get a head start on your armor today."

Liborius shrugged. "No worries. The bread is almost done. Eat first, and then go about your tasks. Speaking of tasks, I already fetched the water this morning. Your lady friends say hello, and they are still puzzling over your last riddle you gave them."

Ailean gave a huffling laugh. "They will never guess the latest one."

Liborius gave a devilish grin. "I'm sure they will not."

The men ate, and then Ailean went to work polishing the metal strips of Liborius's armor. Ailean did not feel right. He felt like his whole body had been beaten, and every small movement caused some muscle or bone to ache. He worked for a few hours and then took a break in the afternoon. Liborius was not home. *Probably on a walk,* he thought to himself. He went to check on the donkey in the stable. She greeted him with her large, dark, round eyes. Her ears pricked, and she moved slowly to Ailean. Ailean petted the donkey. "So I guess you're called Abigail. I would have named you something else, maybe Adina for your gentleness or Anika for your beauty." Ailean smiled. He gave her a good going-over with a brush and made sure she had plenty of food available. He was just leaving the stable when a flash of pain hit him. Abruptly, he was on his knees, head down, supporting himself with one hand on the ground. *Not again,* he thought. *I have too much work to do.* Fighting through the weakness, he stood up and went to finish the armor.

A few days passed, and Ailean continued to come down further with illness. His weakness shortened his walks with Liborius. He was unable to keep any food down and lost a lot of weight. There was a feeling in Ailean's gut that said something was wrong, but he tried to ignore it and hide it from Liborius as best he could. Liborius became increasingly concerned and was not fooled. One morning, Ailean was unable to rise from bed. He was shivering violently in the warm room. Liborius went to check on him.

"I'm tired. I just need a little extra rest," Ailean lied. Ailean tried to fake strength, but there was no hiding the cold sweat that glistened on his sluggish body. His eyes were sunken, and his skin was pale. Everything ached. Liborius laid his hand lightly on Ailean's shoulder, and Ailean was soothed by it.

Liborius left his hand there and spoke with a soft voice, "You are not fooling anyone, my friend. You are ill of something. I will fetch a physician right away. You are to remain in bed. No work until you recover."

Liborius immediately departed to find a physician. He turned to his neighbors for recommendation, and they told him where to find Luke. Luke was a Hellenistic Jew. Hellenistic Judaism was a form of Judaism in classical antiquity that combined Jewish religious tradition with elements of Greek culture and wisdom. Luke's neighbors did not agree with his religious views but respected his work as a healer. He had traveled a good distance, probably from Troas, the province where ancient Troy was said to be, to visit a friend who was not well and was staying in Capernaum to heal him. But he made his services available to those in need.

Luke was a young man with eyes that showed wisdom beyond his age. His young forehead was thinning and raised in fine wrinkles. Some folks wear a smile, but Luke radiated a smile. His accent was a beautiful, playful tune as if he were in a play. Everything about him was a soft and understated joy as he greeted Liborius and asked to see Ailean immediately. Luke was taken to Ailean. Ailean's face had an unhealthy look to it, and his eyes were hard open as he stared at nothing on the wall. Luke came over in fast, easy strides to the bed and gently squeezed Ailean's hand.

"I see you are not well. Tell me all the areas that hurt." Luke gave Ailean a thorough examination. After the prodding was done, he took Liborius aside to talk. He promised to make Ailean more comfortable and told Liborius that unfortunately, there was not much he could do. He had seen this illness before, and whatever afflicted Ailean would not improve.

Ailean thanked Luke for his visit and offered payment to the physician, but Luke refused. Liborius escorted Luke out and watched as he walked away and out of sight. The weight in Liborius's chest was heavy as he contemplated what to do for his friend. He returned to Ailean, who was asleep in bed. Liborius prayed.

CHAPTER XXI

FAITH

Liborius heard that a large crowd had already gathered at a plain on a mountainside just outside Capernaum to hear Jesus speak. Ailean would not be able to travel. His condition continued to worsen. Ailean, his face as pale as a cloud, continued to rest in bed. Liborius was worried for his friend and refused to leave him to see the great rabbi teach, but Ailean insisted.

"I have served with loyalty for many years and have never asked for anything," Ailean entreated. "Though I served, I have loved you like a brother. I ask you to do this for me as if this were my last request." Ailean, his eyes filled with laughter lines—he who was often happy—was deadly serious at that moment.

Liborius sighed and then departed alone to hear Jesus. Fearing that he would miss the rabbi, he grabbed his cloak quickly and ran out the door. He was in great physical condition and moved with purpose. His cloak billowed in the dry, cool breeze as he hurried. It did not take long to reach the bottom of the mountainside. A great multitude of people was moving. He followed.

As he walked up the steep incline, his breath was taken for a second as he noticed Abigail and Nathan trudging up the hill. Abigail was beautiful, more beautiful than he remembered. His face split into a grin, and he pushed through the crowd to meet them. "Abigail!" he shouted.

Abigail stopped and turned to Liborius. Her eyes drew close. "Well, centurion, you will not delay me this time," she said with mock sternness and then smiled. "I have traveled a good distance to hear Jesus speak. I have heard his words before, so powerful every time I listen to him that it's like hearing him for the first time. I'm sure you will not be disappointed that you came."

She then ignored Liborius and moved quickly with Nathan close by. Liborius followed them into the flock of people. They came upon a large crowd of Jesus's disciples with a great multiple of people from all over Judea, from Jerusalem and as far as the coasts of Tyre and Sidon, to listen to Jesus. Many came to be healed of their diseases and delivered from demonic spirits.

Jesus was already speaking. Liborius studied the rabbi. Jesus wore a simple tunic made of one piece of cloth and sandals. His features were similar to others in the region. He had penetrating brown eyes, dark brown hair not very long but a little scruffy, and olive-brown skin. He was not tall and stood about 5 feet 5 inches, an average man's height. His voice was not loud, but the mountain seemed to amplify his words—words that were powerful and novel, astonishing words that told of loving your enemies and even blessing those who curse you. Liborius stared in awe, wondering how one so plain-spoken and unembellished could achieve this level of wisdom.

The crowd listened to many parables. In one of the notable parables, Jesus uttered, "Why do you look at the speck of sawdust in your brother's eye and pay no attention to the plank in your own eye?"[1] In this parable, Jesus warned not to be a hypocrite and

---

1. Matt. 7:3

explained, "First take the plank out of your eye, and then you will see clearly to remove the speck from your brother's eye."[2] He said it is foolish to criticize someone for a fault while remaining blind to our own considerable faults. He taught that we are generally far more tolerant of our own sins than we are of the sins of others.

Liborius had never heard such radical thoughts, and he was moved by the words of Jesus. He recognized that Jesus spoke with true authority. The people were amazed as Jesus began to heal. Those troubled by evil spirits were cured, and all the people who touched Jesus were healed by his power. Liborius regretted not bringing Ailean to be healed. If only he had known, he would have carried Ailean to meet Jesus. A single tear slid down his cheek at the thought. Liborius felt hollow and empty, a proud Roman centurion known for strength reduced to weakness and fear.

After Jesus departed, the large crowd slowly walked away. Liborius wanted to find and talk with Jesus, but he was nervous. He was anguished about whether a non-Jew, called a Gentile, who was also a sinner according to the Torah, would be granted an audience with this popular rabbi. Instead, he decided to say his goodbyes to Abigail and Nathan. He did not have to search long. He felt a slight touch on his back. It was Nathan.

"I see you are not in uniform today. I could barely recognize you."

Liborius replied, "No work today, my friend. I barely recognized you. You're growing like a weed."

Nathan tilted his head to the sky, pretending to grow. Abigail rolled her eyes. "My son, a growing weed? More than likely, he will be shorter than most. More like a growing seedling." Nathan frowned.

Liborius turned toward Abigail. "You are a lovely flower that grows more beautiful each day." Abigail's cheeks turned red.

---

2. Matt. 7:5

"You know, the boy looks up to you," she interrupted. "I see him waving sticks like he is a warrior of Rome. He hit a friend a bit too hard. He paid for that one." Nathan instinctively touched his rear. "We must be on our way back to Genneseret. If you are ever that way, please stop by and visit Nathan. Maybe you can teach him something more useful than waving sticks."

Liborius smiled at the invitation. He wanted to escort them back to Genneseret now but could not forget Ailean suffering in bed. They said their goodbyes, and Liborius watched them depart.

Liborius traveled immediately back home, concerned for the well-being of his servant and wanting to tell him all he had heard and seen. Unfortunately, Ailean had taken a serious turn for the worse and was close to death when Liborius arrived. He could barely hear Liborius talking with him. All he felt, all he knew was the pain of that moment. Liborius was beside himself with grief for his dear friend. Though Liborius had not met Jesus in person, Jesus became his hope. Jesus was probably still in Capernaum. Liborius did not feel worthy enough to approach Jesus. He reached out immediately to some elders of the synagogue to go on his behalf and ask Jesus to heal his servant. He sent this message: "Lord, my servant is lying paralyzed at home, suffering terribly." These elders had no issue with the ministry of Jesus and respected Liborius as a friend of the Jews. They agreed to approach Jesus for his sake. They left immediately and pleaded with Jesus earnestly. They presented Liborius as "deserving" because of his work for the Jewish people, especially the synagogue he had built. Jesus spoke with the elders and agreed to help, simply because he was asked. Prestige or works never influenced who he healed.

Liborius was happy to hear that Jesus would come but felt that it might be a problem for the prominent rabbi to come into his home, so he sent his friends to say to him:

Lord, I am not good enough for you to come into my house. You need only to give the order, and my servant will be

*healed. I know this because I understand authority. There
are people who have authority over me, and I have soldiers
under my authority. I tell one soldier, "Go," and he goes.
I tell another soldier, "Come," and he comes. I say to my
servant, "Do this," and my servant obeys me.*[3]

Jesus was amazed when he heard this and said:

*The truth is, this man has more faith than anyone I have
found, even in Israel. Many people will come from the
east and from the west. These people will sit and eat with
Abraham, Isaac, and Jacob in God's kingdom. And those
who should have the kingdom will be thrown out. They will
be thrown outside into the darkness, where people will cry
and grind their teeth with pain.*[4]

After Jesus spoke, the men who had been sent returned to the
home of Liborius.

Liborius sat near Ailean waiting for his friends to return to the
house. Death was coming soon. Liborius knew that. Death took
where it could, taking people far too early, far too good. It didn't
pretend to discriminate. Ailean had closed his eyes a few hours ago.
Liborius watched the rise and fall of Ailean's chest, waiting for his
last breath. Ailean suddenly took a big breath, and after he exhaled,
his eyes opened. Strength returned to his face, and Liborius watched
as Ailean was miraculously healed. Liborius wept with happiness
and praised openly the God of the Jews for the miracle. The friends
who were sent returned and found Ailean well. Ailean was beyond
well, talking and laughing again. They told Liborius and Ailean all
that took place in the meeting with Jesus. Everyone gave thanks and
praised God.

3. Matt. 8:8–9 ERV
4. Matt. 8:10–12 ERV

EPILOGUE

Today, the words of the centurion are used in prayer in churches around the world. The story of the centurion's faith is important today, maybe now more than ever. We live in a cynical world filled with harsh realities, as well as unfaithful and selfish people. The modern age we live in is filled with distractions and temptations. Yes, there were distractions and temptations in the past, but with technology, everything has changed. Technology, the works of human hands, pleases our senses, our inflated egos, and makes us feel like we can do almost anything. There are blessings of technology such as health sciences, but it can be a curse creating an illusion of eternal bliss. Technology for some becomes their faith and replaces faith in God. It is the idol requiring no faith. Regardless of what is seen, heard, experienced, or hoped, faith is the only means of hope and salvation.

In this novel, many historic events were described. Similar events are played out and repeated today. The mistakes of history are constantly repeated. Think about why this is the case. Will humanity ever learn? We are such sinful creations. I admit that there are times when one should forget the past and move on, but the lessons of the past always need to be heeded. Sounds easy, doesn't it? Yet people constantly disappoint, for that is our nature. People are sheep who need a good shepherd. A shepherd has been provided to us if we will only listen.

The character Liborius was a dreamer. I would like to give some important advice. Don't give up on your dreams. Never give up batting, even though you're in a slump. The next toss of the ball may be a hit. Do not listen to the naysayers. Continue to dream always and often. A tip for success is to visualize those dreams into goals. If you focus and keep visualizing those dreams, you can reach your goals. Don't believe anyone who tells you that something can't be done. They will never believe in you until you prove them wrong. There may be hardships ahead, but it is hardships that define us and make us better. You have to stand up and take action for yourself. The world will always need dreamers. Senator Robert F. Kennedy liked to quote George Bernard Shaw, and in his 1968 campaign for president, he said this about dreaming: "You see things; and you say "Why?" But I dream things that never were; and I say "Why not?"[1]

I hope you found the humor added to this book. Having a good sense of humor may provide many health benefits. It reduces stress, helps you cope with pain, creates empathy in social situations, and is one of the cures for anxiety. As children, we laugh hundreds of times a day, but as adults, we rarely do. In seeking out more opportunities for humor, we can improve our emotional health, strengthen our friendships, and find greater happiness. We might even add years to our lives. Always remember to try to find the humor in things. Funny things do happen in your everyday life. So if you're having a bad day, crack a smile anyway.

If you are not a Christian, please think of joining a church. You will find fellowship in a community where acceptance and forgiveness are found, a place of healing and restoration, a place of nurture and growth, a place of belonging, a place of prayer.

Finally, I would like to leave you my favorite Bible verses.

---

1. *Respectfully Quoted: A Dictionary of Quotations*, 1989, *Bartleby.com*, https://www.bartleby.com/73/465.html.

Therefore I tell you, do not worry about your life, what you will eat or drink; or about your body, what you will wear. Is not life more than food, and the body more than clothes? Look at the birds of the air; they do not sow or reap or store away in barns, and yet your heavenly Father feeds them. Are you not much more valuable than they? Can any one of you by worrying add a single hour to your life?

And why do you worry about clothes? See how the flowers of the field grow. They do not labor or spin. Yet I tell you that not even Solomon in all his splendor was dressed like one of these. If that is how God clothes the grass of the field, which is here today and tomorrow is thrown into the fire, will he not much more clothe you—you of little faith? So do not worry, saying, 'What shall we eat?' or 'What shall we drink?' or 'What shall we wear?' For the pagans run after all these things, and your heavenly Father knows that you need them. But seek first his kingdom and his righteousness, and all these things will be given to you as well. Therefore do not worry about tomorrow, for tomorrow will worry about itself. Each day has enough trouble of its own.

—Matt. 6:25–34

SOURCES

Casson, Lionel. *The Ancient Mariners*. Princeton, NJ: Princeton University Press, 1991.

Dando-Collins, Stephen. *Caesar's Legion: The Epic Saga of Julius Caesar's Elite Tenth Legion and the Armies of Rome*. Hoboken, NJ: John Wiley & Sons, 2002.

Gelb, Norman. *Herod the Great: Statesman, Visionary, Tyrant*. Lanham, MD: Rowman & Littlefield Publishing Group, 2013.

Loffreda, Stanislao. *Capharnaum: The Town of Jesus*. Jerusalem: Franciscan Printing Press, 1985.

———. *Recovering Capharnaum*. Jerusalem: Franciscan Printing Press, 1985.

Oleson, John Peter. *The Oxford Handbook of Engineering and Technology in the Classical World*. Oxford: Oxford University Press, 2009.

Plutarch, Lucius Mestrius. "Caesar at Long Last Distributed the Booty." Caesar 55, Loeb Classical Library, 1919.

———. "Caesar Staged No Fewer Than Four Triumphs." Caesar 65, Loeb Classical Library, 1919.

———. "The Festival of the Lupercalia." Caesar 61, Loeb Classical Library, 1919.

———. *Plutarch's Lives of Illustrious Men*, Vol. 2. New York: John B. Alden Publisher, 1887. 543, Google Books.

————. "Let the Dice Fly High." Caesar 32, Loeb Classical Library, 1919.

————. "Yes the Ides Have Come, but Not Yet Passed." Caesar 63, Loeb Classical Library, 1919.

Secundus, Gaius Plinius. *Pliny the Elder, The Natural History*. London: Penguin Classics, 1991.

Tacitus, Cornelius. *The Annals*, Trans. by Michael Grant. London: The Folio Society, 2006.

————. *The Histories*, Volumes 1 and 2. Oxford: Oxford University Press, 1980.

Tranquillus, C. Suetonius. *The Lives of the Twelve Caesars*. Ware, Hertfordshire: Wordsworth Editions, 1997.

————. *The Twelve Caesars*. Translated by Robert Graves. West Sussex, UK: Allen Lane, 1979.

SPECIAL THANKS

Special thanks to the works of ancient historians Suetonius Tranquillus, Plutarch, Lucius Mestrius, and Gaius Cornelius Tacitus, all major sources from the period of Julius Caesar to Domitian. They include vivid details of the emperors' characters and habits and quotes from a variety of sources, including official and private documents and gossip of the time.